Praise for *The Book of the Dun Cow*

"Far and away the most literate
Mr. Wangerin's allegorical fantas
good and evil produces a reson
reverberates in memory."

—New York Times

"Belongs on the shelf with Animal Farm, Watership Down and The Lord of the Rings. It is, like them, an absorbing, fanciful parade of the war between good and evil. A powerful and enjoyable work of the imagination."

—Los Angeles Times

"Good and evil were never seen more distinctly not pitted more ferociously than in this animal fable, reverberating with the righteousness of the Bible or a medieval morality play ... The animals are not mere literary symbols but are invested with a humanness all their won."

—The Saturday Evening Post

"Wangerin's story functions as a frightening representation of modern evil ... a parable for adults to ponder."

—The Christian Century

"Wangerin has so fluidly woven all these legends together into one small gem."

—Washington Post Book World

Praise for *The Second Book of the Dun Cow: Lamentations*

"[A] profoundly imagined and beautifully stylized fable of the immemorial war between good and evil."

—The New York Times

"A beautifully written fantasy anchored starkly in reality."

–The Washington Post

"[A] fine book about the way evil enters the world, and this newly told story of Chaunticleer is one that details the loss of his innocence, of his love and of his God."

—The Houston Chronicle

To my friend Larry Bamesberger,
A man most intimate with mouths

Diversion Books
A Division of Diversion Publishing Corp.
443 Park Avenue South, Suite 1004
New York, New York 10016
www.DiversionBooks.com

For more information, email info@diversionbooks.com

First Diversion Books edition June 2013.

Print ISBN: 978-1-62681-260-4
eBook ISBN: 978-1-62681-103-4

The Second Book of the Dun Cow

Lamentations

Walter Wangerin Jr.

DIVERSIONBOOKS

A REPRISE

Two Chapters from the
First Book of the Dun Cow

[Twenty-Seven]
"A Dog with no Elusion"— the last Battle, the War

"Sum Wyrm, sub terra!" *The voice seethed from the restless river. From the ground around the camp (where the Animals shrank in terror), from the forest, and from all the the lands beyond, the voice echoed and reechoed as if the whole earth were a drum thundering. The battlement wall was shaken by the sound: parts of it cracked, other parts crumbled. It seemed to Chauntecleer that he was hearing the voice through the very tembling beneath his feet.*

"Sum Wyrm, sub terra. Once, Chauntecleer, you had an opportunity," *the voice roared.* "But you have squandered it. Your opportunity is lost."

This voice was legion—a chorus of voices, a thousand choirs chanting all around his head: "I am Wyrm from underneath the earth, coming, coming! I mean to be free!"

The little Rooster on the top of the battlement and facing the sea, Chauntecleer, in the grip of his wife Pertelote, began to shriek, "Come, snake! O viper, come! I don't care! I don't care anymore! This is the way that it ends!"

The shaking of the earth grew more violent. Whole sections of the battlemen wall slipped sideways, broke into great, tumbling chunks; and then there were gaps in the wall. A mysterious confusion struck the waves of the sea south. Instead of their rhythmic rolling toward the camp, there was a dizzy turning. They slapped and struggled against one another, giants without direction, enormous hands clapping.

Chauntecleer jerked against Pertelote's hold, writhed in her wings.

"Why not?" he screamed as the breach in the wall came very close. Soon he and Pertelote were on a narrow pedestal, and nowhere to go. "Why not? This is the way that it should be, Wyrm! It is all, all of it, falling apart!" In spite of his broken body, he doubled his effort to tear himself out of Pertelote's grip. And he would have slashed her, if he could.

But a ponderous growl ascended from the river—a new sound—and then the very earth sprang back.

Chauntecleer was thunderstruck.

As if the earth had a mouth, as if that mouth were yawning, a chasm had opened up where once there was a battlefield. The pedestal, the whole camp, moved backward slowly, as if in reverence before this hole, to give it space. Suddenly Chauntecleer and Pertelote were on the edge of an abysmal cliff, while across the chasm the other edge was hidden by the torrents of water falling into it. The crack in the earth knifed both left and right, as far as the eye could see—and the gorge was widening. The mantle of the earth had split!

"Sum Wyrm, sub terra!"

The voice was greater than the roaring of the waterfall—a falls with no ending east nor west. The chasm was drinking the sea before it, and the sea rushed in it like suicide. But ever farther did the sea and the falls spead from the Rooster and the Hen beside him. The gorge was widening still.

"Coming, coming! I mean to be free!"

Now, for the first time, this great voice arose from a single source. All in spite of himself Chauntecleer found that he was bending forward to peer into the bottom of the chasm. As he did he felt as if he were high in the air and in danger for his life. But he looked to find the voice.

"Wyrm," he whispered. But still he saw nothing. He saw the waters cascade and boil at the bottom. He saw mud sliding down the nearer wall and stones spinning past the mud, down and down deeper than the pits of God.

Then the bottom of the gorge convulsed, rumpled—and in a moment the odor of rot fulminated in Chauntecleer's face. He lost footing. Unconsciously he reached for Pertelote and buried his face in the feathers at her throat. Her scent was sweet. Pertelote touched him at his shoulder. The Rooster swallowed twice and wept—ashamed.

"No good!" *The voice from the pit, frightening in its clarity.* "Who knows the nostrils better than I? I am conimg, coming! I mean to be free!"

Without releasing Pertelote, Chauntecleer looked down again to the bottom, and the he did: he saw great Wyrm.

Slowly easing itself between the lower jaws of the pit was a long black body of horrible size. Neither head nor tail, neither beginning nor end could be seen, for they passed miles and miles away through the caverns of the earth. He saw the surface of the monster's flesh, for its greater bulk lodged yet deeper than the bottom. The body was turning like a rolling mill, turning, sloughing huge fields of rotting flesh—and this body was itself the floor of the gorge.

As Wyrm turned, the chasm, the earth crack, grew—a mighty power driving it. And the water, when finally it hit Wyrm's flesh, steamed.

Chauntecleer drew Pertelote to himself and held her in despair.

"The Keepers," *Wyrm bellowed,* "have failed. You all are broken. The earth is breaking. And I shall be free!"

"God forgive me," Chauntecleer breathed.

Pertelote said, "He will. Watch forgiveness: there is one thing left to do."

"What is left?" said the Rooster in an agony.

Their pinnacle tumbled. Chauntecleer leaped and landed and immediately had to race back from the collapsing ground. Sections of the camp itself began to fall into the chasm. The earth along the edge of it simply gave up and slumped the near side down.

"What is left?" cried Chauntecleer, clawing at his breast. For the Coop nodded drunkenly over the edge of the precipice. Then its back end lifted off the ground. It hung on the edge a moment, considering death. Then it tipped over and passed away.

"What?" Chauntecleer screamed as he found himself suddenly next to the eating cliff. "Pertelote, what?"

A long time the Coop spun downward, until it was tiny—until like a dry leaf it landed on Wyrm's flesh, and flashed into flame.

"WYRM!"

Who was that? Who called the name with such a piercing conviction? Chauntecleer looked up and stared wildly about.

The Animals were mewling north, just short of the forest, frantic at the disappearance of the ground, one Animal squirming under another's belly, making an ingrown knot of themselves.

"WYRM!" that fearless cry. "Can evil look upon a Dog?"

Not from the Animals! But running in a shaggy, loping, easy gait along the lip of the chasm, never missing a step, drooping his nose over into the vile depths, was Mundo Cani Dog, far west of the Rooster!

"Wyrm, look at me! Wyrm, see me! A Dog! A Dog! A nothing to look upon!"

Chauntecleer saw the rotting body cease turning. Wyrm, wound through the caverns of the earth, held still.

"A Dog is going to fight with you!"

Chauntecleer shot a narrow look at this Dog. Fight with him! For God's sake, Mundo Cani!

Then a closer look and recognition: Mundo Cani was carrying a weapon. Wood, it seemed, like any other bleached branch, but curved and dangerously sharp. Or bone brought to a lethal point. Or this: it looked exactly like the lost horn of the Dun Cow.

"O Wyrm! O Wyrm!" Mundo Cani challenged Evil in a ringing,

imperative bark. Lightly he ran along the wasting cliff, dancing away from the chunks that nodded and tumbled in. Mundo Cani had a talent.

"Great Wyrm is afraid to look at a nothing? A nose, a flea? Wyrm fears to see the speck that calls him out? Such mightiness wants to hide from a Dog? WYRM," Mundo Cani cried to high heaven and into earth, to all the regions underneath the earth, cried, "WYRM!"

Chauntecleer cast a glance at Pertelote. Had she expected this? Was this the thing left to do?

When he looked at her he saw that she too was huddled, covering her face and her eyes and her ears against the good Dog's lonely game.

The Rooster's heart split. He began to gather dust and throw it upon himself. The high, thin wail of grief and guilt rose from his chest and filled the air.

"Oh, my God," Chauntecleer wept.

"Wyrm! Wyrm! Wyrm!" Mundo Cani was sneering. Like needles he sent the utmost scorn down into the pit. He was running the edge of it far away from Chauntecleer.

Then the monstrous body below began to move again. Not turning this time, but with a new purpose sliding straight through the crevice, bunching and sliding, bunching and sliding.

"A Dog is going to fight with you! Of all the noble, a Dog is chosen. Look at me Wyrm—and see yourself!" Mundo Cani swung the horn in wild arcs. "But look! O Wyrm, look at me!"

Then, deep in the gorge, thrusting itself out of stone, out of God's dungeons, there came a single, steady eye.

A glistering orb, unblinking, lidless and looking, that cold eye. Wyrm's eye. White around black, and black so black that all the hosts of night might enter there and never be found again.

Mundo Cani had his wish. Wyrm was looking at him.

For an instant Mundo Cani crouched, taut upon the cliff, the long horn between his teeth. Then, with a triumphant howl, he leaped.

Over the edge, past the mud, missing the rock like a shadow, down and down Mundo Cani descended, the white horn livid.

Wyrm's eye had almost begun to turn. But Mundo Cani had aimed himself well, had made a cross-bow bolt of his fall. He hit the eye hard, with all four feet. He scrambled, grabbed a footing with his sharp claws, raised the horn, and drove its butt through the white flesh.

How Wyrm raged then!

Back and forth the body slammed against the sides of the canyon. Roarings ascended, as if the caverns of the earth were all Wyrm's throat, filled with hideous dismay. No longer was his vast motion controlled. Evil went mad—and blind.

Now the far side of the chasm began to crumble altogether. Boulders hurtled into the deep. The streaming water gouged the cliff face, gouged the weaker parts and vomited rock. Soon the whole wall collapsed inward. The sea above simply stumbled, as if surprised in its forward motion by the drop-off. It stumbled, then settled much lower than it had been before. And in a moment—by the mountains of loose earth and by the mixing of the water, forming a strong mortar—the chasm filled, the earth crack closed.

In heaven the clouds ripped asunder like a veil. And the light of the sun plunged down and filled the earth. And Lord Chauntecleer saw. And in a world suddenly silent, suddenly bright, the Rooster grieved.

Behind him: neither Coop nor camp nor wall. A desolation.

In front of him, a sparkling and peaceful sea. And, finally, between him and the waters, an endless scar east to west in the face of the earth—a hard and sterile seam.

It was this scar that the miserable Rooster was watching. But he wasn't seeing it. In his mind, as if the scene were still unfolding, he was watching the immediate past. And this was the sight: as Wyrm was battering the earth-pit, and as the wall was caving in on him, there was a Dog in his eye, stabbing and stabbing with a long horn, shredding that black orb until it was no more, a bloody, sightless socket.

Wyrm, and more than Wyrm—O heavens, witness the calamity!—

that scar had knit Mundo Cani too beneath the earth.

In sunshine Chauntecleer went to Pertelote and lay down next to her.

"Marooned," he said. He buried his face in the flaming feathers of her throat. "Marooned."

[Twenty-Eight]
And the Last Thing Done is Pertelote's Doing

John Wesley Weasel did not die; but it took him a long time to accept that fact.

He had developed an abhorrence for the light. Sunlight made him sick, both in body and in soul, because he should have awoken in death's darkness. He was, after all, a Weasel, and his every Weaselish weakness was intensified during his convalescence. It humiliated him, for he observed how other animals flit glances at his one-eared head and at the hairless scar along his side. It angered him, for the sun had never—never once— shone upon the Wee Widow Mouse when she was alive; but now that she was dead, and now that the sun had no business even to be, it shone with an outrageous glory. For John Wesley Weasel, daylight was a cruel gift, come altogether too late.

As soon as he could walk the Weasel took himself into the darkness. There was no Coop for the shade, no roof for the covering, no floor nor any space beneath a floor for the hiding. Therefore he went back to his old burrow at the base of a maple tree.

"Is no use in it," he said, and he determined never to come out again.

Pertelote heard his remarks. She had been tending to the Weasel all through his physical healing.

"Mice cleans in the spring. What's cleanings to kill for? What's cleanings for taking a house away?"

When, after several days and nights, he neither came out of his burrow nor made another sound inside of it, Pertelote took the problem to Chauntecleer—who dealt with it directly.

"Yo, John!" He set up a clamor from the middle of the flat, empty yard. "John, yo! Wesley, yo! Weasel!"

The Animals whom he had called as troops before the war began— these he sent back to their own homes. Scattered around him now, pecking and working with an afternoon's industry (for it was the middle of the afternoon, and he had crowed the proper canonical crow as ever he had before) were the ten Hens that had survived, and the seven Brothers Mice, orphans after the death of the Wee Widow Mouse, their mother whom John Wesley mourned. The Creatures of Chauntecleer's coop were busy gathering foodstuffs.

"Yo—John!"

There came no answer from the burrow, neither a shift nor a vibration.

"John Wesley! Laggard! Get out! Come here! We are not going to feed you. We'll spend no pity on a fool. And when you've wasted away to bones, we are not going to mourn a blockhead's passing. Get out! Get to work! There's work to be done!"

Work, indeed. A sea to the south of them. Closer than the sea, that scar of a clenched and poisonous soil. And then, between the scar and the forest, an open space which had once been the busy center of Chauntecleer's yard, of the Coop that was and is no more. Work: the Keepers must unify themselves again, must heal, must become a well-knit community, must obey again the cloud-walking God who had from the beginning appointed them by their meek administration to keep Wyrm bound in his prison under the earth.

"It's done, John Wesley," the Rooster crowed. "The time will be ours

again, if we make it so. It's done, and now we must look to the day. It's up to us."

But still, from the burrow beneath the maple, nothing.

Chauntecleer turned to Pertelote. "Okay," he said, "I've no patience left for a mope."

"But grief will kill him."

"That's what he wants, isn't it?"

"Is that what you want?"

"Want! I want my land made new. I want to scrub the past clean out of my soul. I hate it. I want never to think of it for the rest of my life."

"But you can't help thinking about it," Pertelote said. "You can't rid your soul of the thing that has changed you. Chauntecleer: you must pity the Weasel. He's slower to change. For all his bluster, he needed the past and its purpose more that you."

"So you say, woman. But as long as he remembers, as long as he sulks, he forces me to remember. And if I have to forget John Wesley with the past—well, I will. That's the way it is."

"And Mundo Cani?"

"What"—Chauntecleer bristled—"about Mundo Cani?"

"You will forget him too?"

"No!"

But, yes. As a matter of fact, ever since Mundo Cani had conceived the means to turn Wyrm back into his dungeons, Chauntecleer had determined to forget the Dog. There was guilt in that memory. The Dog's noble sacrifice accused the Rooster's failure, which burned like sin in his soul.

And that—how can such contrarieties be explained?—that was the very reason why he found himself praising Mundo Cani to everyone who would listen.

Therefore, Pertelote had not one problem, but two. A Weasel whose present was too much steeped in the past, and a Rooster whose present strove to deny the past. But the Hen of the crimson throat was equal to both her blockheads. And what she did then we might call the last and the best battle of all. Pertelote spoke.

Chauntecleer had a dread of the Netherworld scar. As long as he slept ground-level with it, the scar hectored his dreams.

So Pertelote wondered out loud whether there wasn't some branch above the ground where he and she could roost more peacefully.

Awake and trembling, Chauntecleer lifted his eye and saw a single standing maple tree. Well, if he had surrendered Lordship in one great thing, he could at least be Lord over the little things. He led his Animals to the maple.

In the evening Chauntecleer crowed both vespers and compline in manners appropriate to the times. It settled ten Hens on lower branches. They began then to patter the ground below. That is to say, they flipped their tails, dropped damp plops, and ruffled their feathers like like blankets for sleeping. Which is to say, they relieved themselves as Hens had always relieved themselves, but with this difference, that they dropped slops around the burrow of a Weasel and into it, making for a very sour sulk.

Pertelote heard a series of sneezes (and minor curse words) arising from a Weasel's hole.

With some heat she said, "Mundo Cani!"

Chauntecleer loved sleep. It irritated him to be awoken.

"Mundo Cani," Pertelote repeated. "The most glorious Dog!"

"What?" Chauntecleer snorted. "What?"

"Mundo Cani," she said. "Nothing more. Good night."

Now Chauntecleer could not go back to sleep. Pertelote's tone had been curt, forbidding. He tried various positions, shaking the limb heartily, giving the Hen herself something to think about.

Finally he snapped, "Mundo Cani—and what?"

"He's on your mind."

"No! He is not on my mind."

A Weasel at the root of the maple sneezed and began to rub his nose violently.

"No," she said. "Of course he's not on your mind. Why should he be?"

"He is too on my mind!"

"Of course he is."

"I haven't forgotten him, if that's what you mean."

"Right. You memorialize him."

"But I don't dwell on him."

"Of course not. The past is the past."

"Right!"

For an instant the Rooster felt he'd won the argument. In the next instant he wasn't so sure. Memories of Mundo Cani hurt and humbled him.

"Pertelote?"

"Chauntecleer?"

"I miss him." The Rooster spoke softly. "I miss him—terribly."

"Oh, my Lord, I know that."

She too had softened her words. For a moment she added nothing more because she wanted to hear her husband speak. She let his thoughts eat away at his soul.

Wise was the beautiful Hen. She broke her silence. "Perhaps you see the Dog plunging his weapon into the jelly-flesh of Wyrm's eye."

"Oh, Pertelote." Chauntecleer remembered the last words the Dun Cow spoke to him: Moricae fidei. You of little faith, it has been all for you.

Wretchedly, the Rooster murmured, "It should have been me. I should have gone down into the pit. I should have died, not Mundo Cani."

"Even so," said Pertelote. "And what else?"

"I was the Lord of the Coop. It was my duty. I am not right. Today is not right. Tonight and tomorrow…." he said. "I have no right to life."

"And this is why you work so hard these days?"

"I don't know."

"To busy yourself? To pay him back by breaking yourself? What else, Chauntecleer."

"What else? A leader lost and a Dog took over. A leader lives to be sick of living. What else do you want?"

"What else do you owe the hero Mundo Cani?"

"My life! Dammit, I have already said it!"

"Penance."

"What?"

"Penance. This is more than your life. Are you able to scrub the past from your soul? Forgiveness, sweet Chauntecleer, can cleanse your soul. This would be your deliverance. Honor the worth of Mundo Cani's life. Confess your transgression. A Dog will forgive you."

"I have confessed!"

"Oh, Chauntecleer, he knew he had to go down. Don't you understand? There never was a question about who must make the sacrifice. Leader or not, it just wasn't your place to go. You had killed the Cockatrice. That was yours. But Wyrm's eye was Mundo Cani's. With neither fear nor hesitation, he knew what was required of him. He accepted his destiny. His last act was not your deepest transgression. If you keep swaddling yourself in the guilt of your lesser transgression, you deny the greater. Penance for what, Chauntecleer? Say it."

"Oh, Pertelote, stop."

"Say it!"

"I can't."

"But you know it?"

"Yes."

"Then say it."

Chauntecleer could say it in a hole, perhaps. But to speak the thing to his wife? To risk judgment and the loss of her love—?

Chauntecleer said, "I despised him."

"You despised him even while he was making ready to save us all."

"I cursed him as a traitor."

"You did."

"I did."

"Thank you. God bless you, my husband. Saying so is the beginning of a new life. And saying so to Mundo Cani himself will be the ending of the old."

Side by side in the clear, star-sandy night, feeling breezes blowing hither from the sea, they sat on the limb of the maple in silence, the Hen placidly, the Rooster miserably.

Pertelote touched his shoulder.

He shivered.

"Chauntecleer?" she said.

He knew no other word to say. He said nothing.

Pertelote said, "I love you."

"Ahhhhhh."

Shortly before the morning broke, something began to tug at Chauntecleer's mind. Something Pertelote had said, but which must, it seemed to him, be impossible.

"Whoa! You said I should confess the thing to Mundo Cani? Pertelote! Mundo Cani is shut underneath the earth!"

"He was that. The Netherworld Scar is a fearsome closing."

"The Dog is dead."

"You know this for a fact? What if he is alive? What if he is a living, clawing cur in the flesh of mighty Wyrm? What then? He had a nose for intuition. Only the bravest," she said, "can go to him and see him again. Perhaps it will be you, my Lord." She increased the volume of her voice and sang out: "I doubt that a Weasel has the stuff of bravery."

"What?" A little word burped in a stinking burrow.

"Because a Weasel has given up."

"What?"

"The Weasel has buried himself in his own little hidey hole, which is *about as deep as a Weasel can go, nothing as deep as the tunnel that can lead bravery into the dungeons where Wyrm hides."*

"What? What?"

"No more adventures for a Weasel with half a head—"

And now a clamoring bubbled out of the burrow: "Double-u's, they isn't Double-u's on account of their ears! John mourns a Mouse, you cut-cackle! But John can find tunnels better'n any Roster can. Ha! And ha, ha!"

"Because Mundo Cani was never anything to a Weasel but a carriage to carry him about. No friendship—"

"Ha, ha, ha!" cried John Wesley. "What does a Hen think about that?"

Chauntecleer ruffled his feather and let out a crow, "One more 'Ha,' John, and I'll have your last ear for my pocketbook!"

Dawn glowed on the horizon. Hens began to wake.

"A Double-u, he's a Dog's friend too. Is more love in a Weasel than in a Rooster!" John popped up and stood erect beside his burrow.

Chauntecleer leaned dangerously forward to spit his opinions at the Weasel. "You lost no love for him when he saved you!" thundered the Rooster. "I didn't hear a Thank you then!"

John spun in circles, so mad was he. "Speaks a Rooster, ha! A Rooster what was in a Dog's mouth too. Ha, ha, to you, Rooster. Is Double-u's what digs, but Roosters only flutter-gut about. Thinks a Rooster, he can find the Netherworld without a digger to dig?"

"Just wait, you slow mope. I'll find the tunnel before you scratch a grass-root!"

"Ha!"

As it happened then, at sunrise Pertelote spread her wings and sailed down calling her sister Hens to follow—while the adversaries held lively conversation with one another, pointing out the absurdities in each other's characters, and promising mighty promises, each to be fulfilled at an early date.

But the sounds of their bombastic chatter was music in Pertelote's ears. She had been successful. Such contention was good after all. A Weasel and a Rooster were doing what they had always done, and order was restored.

Here Begins the Book of Lamentations

PART ONE

Russel, the Fox
of Good Sense

[One]
In which the Fox Strives to Talk

Russel had fought as bravely as any other Creature in the battle against Wyrm and all his evil Basilisks. Serpents were the Basilisks, three feet long, as black as licorice, thick and dimpled when they writhed. They crawled the ground like little kings with their heads raised up on the loops of their necks. Their eyes were fiery and their flesh moist with poisons. Russel had dashed among them, cutting sharp corners with the snap of his bushy tail, talking, talking, challenging the enemies with a babble of well-constructed sentences. The Fox had rolled in the oils of the rue plant whose stench caused the Basilisks to tighten into helpless balls.

"I route, not to say *route* you by the tens and the twenties, for I am clever and hearty and vulpine, am I!"

But then he bit a fat Basilisk. His canaines burst the serpent, and the serpent wrapped itself round the Fox's snout, and though the Fox dispatched it altogether, its poisons burned him, mouth and tongue and lips and his pointy nose back to the eyeballs—and that was that for Russel's hostilities.

He rubbed his snout with the joints in his forepaws, but only succeeded in smearing the poisons deeper and deeper into his fur, down to the flesh, and then it was that all the flesh of his face stung and, because of his furious rubbing, began to bleed.

"No pity," Russel managed to say. "No cause to pity a Fox, because his wounds, O dear Lord Chauntecleer, they are the wounds of his own folly." Blood scored the gaps between the Fox's teeth. But he could not stop talking. His words sprayed mists of blood. His sentences stretched and wracked his lips. But his love of talk was greater than his pain. For Russel, to talk was to be alive—was to *be*. By talk he had taught tricks to Pertelote's three little Chicks. By talk he had instructed Mice in the ways of Coop-life. Russel was ever a charming orator.

"Fight on," he called to the warrior Creatures of the Coop. "Glorify the day, and triumph by the moonlight!"

Then, when the war had indeed been won, the beautiful Hen Pertelote found the Fox lying inert in the grass, his jaws and his mouth and his muzzle swollen and hardening. Puss and a watery blood seeped through the scabs.

"Russel," Pertelote said with genuine compassion. "What did they do to you?"

The Fox rolled his eyes up to the Hen. He said, "Umph," and "Pumffel."

"Don't talk," she said. "I'll get some salve for—"

Russel said, "No pity, not to say pity, for a Fox who lost good sense."

When he spoke the scabs cracked and the blood gushed.

"Please!" Pertelote begged, wiping the blood with her white wings. "Don't talk! You'll infect yourself."

"All is well," Russel said. "Everything is well. The victory, why, the victory—"

Chauntecleer crowed, "Shut up, you idiot! What's the matter with you?" He leaped into the air, beat his wings, and alighted directly in front of Russel's nose. "Do you *want* to die?"

"But, you see, if I can't talk, well, that's a sort of dying."

Chauntecleer took the Fox's jaws between his talons and shut them in an iron grip.

By the second week of his convalescence Russel wore a carapace from his eyes to the tip of his nose. "Mmmm!" he mewed, his eyes like boiled eggs. "Mmm. Sss," and "Mm-ffle." Fleas had begun to scurry at the roots of his fur.

Pertelote suffered for the sake of her patient. His snout and his breath were foul in her nose. "Oh, Russel," she said softly in his ear. "We can wait to hear you again. Can't you wait to talk?"

Russel tried to obey. But the word that popped into his brains popped immediately out of his mouth.

He said, "Presenting you with thanksgivings, pretty Pertelote." The carapace cracked. The wounds separated, and Russel's **P**'s (**P**resenting, **P**retty, **P**ertelote) sprayed blood.

Wearily Chantecleer said, "For the love of God, you miserable faucet—shut up."

Two Hens walk in a yellow field: white under the sunlight, pure beneath a deep blue sky.

The one in the lead is adorned with a burst of crimson feathers at her throat. The one who follows is fat. Her comb is vestigial, an abrupt, pinch, surrounded by pink baldness on her skull. She huffs and puffs to keep up. This one thrusts her head forward with every waddling step. Her wings hang loose in order to cool her corpulence. She is drenched with sweat.

"There," says the beautiful Pertelote. She gestures with her beak. "There, Jasper. Do you see it? We've found what we came for."

"See, Missus? Not to be doubting you. Pardon me and all

that—but it ain't no more'n a tree."

"Look beyond the tree. To the green vegetation thick on the ground. There are the medicinals. Let's go."

Pertelote spreads her wings to fly.

Jasper says, "Butt pimples." This is the way the fat Hen swears. "Chicken dribbles. Ain't I already gone gut-weary, Missus?"

Pertelote laughs and sails forward.

Jasper grunts. She generally hates laughter, for she believes that most of it is aimed at her. *Fatty, fatty, two by four....* Jasper is of the opinion that Animals are mean and fully of mockery. *Couldn't get through the kitchen door....* Mockery wants a pecking, for pecking gets respect.

Pertelote calls backward, "And don't I love you, Jasper?"

Well. And so. And all right. The fat Hen is mollified. But unable to make a true flight, she plods after her Missus.

The first patches of the green vegetation is jimson weed. Beyond that is a tough tangle of juniper.

Under the jimson Pertelote looks for dark datura.

Jasper comes behind, cussing. "Goat pee."

Pertelote brings up a warty-green thornapple and tosses it back to Jasper:

Thunk!

"Fox farts."

Suddenly Pertelote pauses. She tips her head, listening. She thinks she heard a rustling under the juniper. She shakes her head and she finds another thornapple and tosses this one too at Jasper.

Thunk!

"Hen's teeth, Missus! Is it for knocking down a sister Hen that you throw bombs at her?"

Pertelote says, "Not bombs, Jasper. Sacred datura. There isn't a stronger Hen than you, nor a better one to carry the medicine back."

"Well, folderol," Jasper swears. "Chicken livers in vinegar juice I say. If that's what you wanted, I'm gone, and no skin off'n my beak." She tucks the thornapples one under each wing and leaves.

Again Pertelote hears the rustling ahead of her. She knows the sound. It fills her with sympathy. Someone has isolated herself. Someone is hiding under the juniper.

Pertelote bends to pick berries. She speaks as if to the air. "The sacred datura will put poor Russel to sleep. And it's the juice of the juniper will bathe his infections."

Picking berries. Picking berries. Giving her hidden sister time to adjust to her coming.

Pertelote begins to sing:

> "My sister, she left us for sorrow,
> Poor sparrow.
> We craved her return by the morrow,
> Black laurel.
> When, when will she come forward?"

Pertelote has made a small heap of berries. She stands and raises her head and sings that first line again, but with one variation: "Chalcedony left me in sorrow."

A thin voice peeps, "Sorrow? Not never did I hope to sorrow my Lady. No, not never."

"Of course not. Chalcedony would never mean to sorrow my heart."

Chalcedony falls silent. Even the rustling ceases. Then she says, "Maybe my Lady can go away now?"

"Oh, my sister, why should I go away?"

Again, a long silence.

When Chalcedony speaks again, her voice is moist with tears. "Private matters. Unhappy matters."

"Lady of Sorrows," Pertelote murmurs, "why are you sad? Perhaps I can comfort you."

Now Chalcedony begins to sob. "Hoo, hoo, hoo."

Pertelote spreads the juniper branches aside. Chalcedony is gaunt. In heaven's name, what has she been doing here, alone?

Then the skinny Hen draws back, and Pertelote sees an egg lying before her.

Chalcedony says, "I'm sorry. I am that, my Lady. I didn't never want to cry."

"Sister! You've begun to bring a child to birth."

"I never couldn't lay another since the Rat kilt the first, and that the first of all I ever made. But I says to my soul, 'And why mayn't Chalcedony be layin' an egg like any other?'"

"A lovely little egg. Unblemished."

"Oh, Lady, oh Lady." The thin Hen gives herself over to heavy sobs and tears. "But I been sittin' broody on my perfect egg weeks and weeks, and the pretty bairn can't hatch. Chalcedony, she's got a motherly heart, but never no baby to mother."

Now Pertelote sits down beside her sorrowful sister and lays a wing over her back.

"It is time," she says. "It is surely time to cry."

[Two]
In which Wyrm Contrives New Strategies for Breaking Free

Now, the Serpent was sly, brutish and powerful and thick through the bowels of the earth. But by his first assault against the Keepers of Evil he had learned that the greater his force the more tightly woven became the Meek of the earth. In the end their silken webbing had refused him his desires. Brute power had left him eyeless and blind. The light had been extinguished.

Nevertheless, the Serpent was more subtle than any Beast on earth. He probed his loss. He studied his defeat. He schooled himself in patience, and contrived another stratagem. Blindness had made his own *body* the prison that now enclosed him, a tighter jail than had been the caverns underground. Oh, his hatred of the Creator was a furnace now. Wyrm contemplated annihilation. Freedom! Freedom—and he would swallow every luminary in the universe. He would blind the cosmos entirely and imprison creation, the handwork of heaven, in a perpetual, illimitable dark.

Hatred engenders guile. Wyrm plotted vengeance, dividing

it into several parts. First, he must test the disposition of the Rooster, the ruler and the union of his Keepers. If at any point Lord Chauntecleer was vulnerable, if there were in him the seed of some mortal sin, some bit of Wyrm's own character, then Evil might enlist him as a confederate for his purposes.

Pass my test, Galle superbe, and I will commit myself to a stratagem from which I can never retreat. It shall be my peril—but it shall be your annihilation.

So rash, so cunning, so courageous, and so heroic was this new thing that—except that it meant the triumph of wickedness—all the generations to come would worship him.

Sum Wyrm, sub terra—such Evil is almost a God.

Upon the Rooster's unconscious signal, Wyrm would initiate his own self-sacrifice.

[Three]
The Trick of the Tail

Chauntecleer crowed Compline:

> By day, O God, you grant your steadfast love,
> And at night your song is with us, a prayer to
> the God of our lives.

To Pertelote beside him he said, "Is Russel sleeping?"

"Yes, he is."

"Will he heal?"

"I pray it. I pray it all the time. But he can't eat asleep. And he can't heal without nourishment."

But Chauntecleer was restless for other reasons that Russel alone. The maple was not a home. It stood solitary in a ravished land, where Animals were aliens.

It's done, John Wesley, Chauntecleer had said to the Weasel before nightfall. *The time is ours again, if we make it so. It's done, and now we must look to the day.*

Good words. Good crows to back them up. But he who shaped the day could not himself partake in such consolation.

It can be recorded with no surprise that the war had bereft the Animals of innocence. They had become realists. But——

now that life seemed so precarious, so rare and precious—
their love for one another grew intense. How solicitous they
were for the sick one's health, and how glad they were in the
morning to find the Fox asleep.

With an earnest, soldierly decorum, the seven Brothers
Mice petted Russel and combed his fur. They made sympathetic
noises in their throats, like: "Ah," and "Too bad," and "Oh,
dear Uncle."

The longer he slept the better he healed.

Pertelote lanced the swellings, then dabbed its discharge.
She probed and pressed the riven flesh, rinsed, washed, and
dressed it several times a day. Little Mice gagged pippingly at
the stench their uncle made, but manfully stayed, and dutifully
brought the Lady Hen mosses for sponging, thorns as surgical
instruments. Pertelote pierced the carapace at his lip, inserted
her beak, and squirted water into the Fox.

Wodenstag Mouse scratched at the rough scabs. He said,
"Lady, do you think he feels this?"

"If he didn't flinch from my thorn, he won't feel your nail."

"No," said Wodenstag. "Not my nail. Do you think he
feels *this?*" He ran tiny hands over Russel's face. "This hardness?"

"Not yet," said Pertelote. But he will when he wakes up."

"Will it hurt him?"

"I expect so. He won't have joy in a wooden mouth."

"Poor Uncle Russel."

"But this is the way he is growing new skin. It will itch.
But he'll live if he doesn't split the scab too soon."

One evening, Freitag, the second youngest Mouse, was
watching the Fox's face when suddenly the right eye flew open.
Freitag gave a *yip* and jumped backward. The eye rolled here
and there, though the Fox moved not a hair.

"Hello?" Freitag whispered. "Uncle, are you in there?"

The eye flashed a moment of recognition, then softened, then the lid came down and closed.

"Whoop!" squealed Freitag. He darted this way and that. "Uncle Russel's better! I saw it! He looked at me!"

But no one else saw what the Mouse had seen. Russel was sleeping. So they too went to roost, listened to another Compline, and slept the night through.

It was noon the following day. Though the rest of the Animals hadn't believed Freitag's happy cries, his brothers did. They were all seven patting Russel when he woke. He shivered. The Mice began to clap their hands. "Lookee! Lookee!" they shouted. Russel heard them. This is how they knew that he heard them: he swung his head in their direction. There was a rictus of grinning on his face. He stood up, then collapsed. He scratched at the ground in order to stand again.

He said, *"Huk."* That was all he said. He eyes swelled with the effort. Then again, *"Huk."*

The Mice cried: "Hooray!"

The Fox started to claw at his scabs.

"Wait!" cried Wodenstag. "Uncle, wait! Lady Pertelote says to keep the scab. The scab is good for you."

Russel stared at Wodenstag, grinning, grinning, striving to open his mouth. He gained his feet. Fleas rushed the flesh beneath his coat. He suppressed the irritations. He nodded his head: *Nephews, nephews, isn't it a pretty day?*

The Mice said to one another, "Uncle wants something."

Russel's eyes seemed to smile. *Yes! Aren't we happy to be together again?*

The Fox went a few steps away, then turned and came back and repeated the steps again. *"Huk, huk."* Oh, how dearly he wanted to talk. *Come! It such a beautiful—not to say, beautiful—day, and I've been waiting, waiting, waiting to show you a new trick.*

Russel walked east. He slewed his steps, but went purposefully east.

The Mice looked at one another.

Also, they looked around and saw no one to whom to tell the wonderful news of the Fox's health and happiness.

So they followed.

Extraordinarily, Russel began to trot. The Mice ran. His bushy tail led them. His crusted nose hung low.

They came to the Liver-brook, the south-running river.

Straightway Russel crouched and plunged his face into the water. Standing on the level bank, he thrashed his whole head left and right, blowing spouts and fountains.

"What a good idea!" Wodenstag cried. "Uncle is washing his face!"

"Ohhh," said his brothers, enlightened.

Then the Fox exploded from the water, shouting, "Nephews! I am so glad, not to mention pleased, that you are here, which is to say, where I am!"

The Brothers Mice jumped up and down. "You're talking," they cried.

"I am! I am indeed!" the Fox laughed. "And soon I will have something to say." The carapace had softened and was pulling apart. Patches like rags were sloughing off.

Russel raised an instructive paw. "The Trick of the Stick!"

In his jaws he picked up a slender branch, then walked backwards he entered the Liver-brook butt-and-tail first, his head held high. Blood pimpled his raw flesh.

"Uncle, please," Wodenstag said, "I don't want to see tricks. I don't want to hear tricks. I don't want my uncle hurt again. Let's go back."

But Russel was consumed with his trick.

Unaware, he rubbed his nose with a paw. Unaware, he

smeared blood through his whiskers, making them spike. Unaware, because his attention was behind himself, where he was sinking into the water up to his neck.

"Yes," he said. Said, "Slowly, now. Foxes have wit," he said. "Wit is tricks. Tricks, good nephews, is the notability of Foxes. Watch!"

"Uncle, please!"

Sonntag, Monstag, Deinstag all took off top speed back to the maple.

"Watch the fleas!"

"Dear Uncle Russel," said Wodenstag". Could we please stop now?"

"The word to love," said Russel, panting, a hectic spin in his eyes.

Indeed, fleas were popping and running ahead of the water, up his back, up his shoulders. "The word to love is *washing!*"

Russel sank completely under the water. Only the stick could be seen. And the stick was covered with a thousand fleas. And then the stick floated away. But Russel himself, he did not surface.

Wodenstag cried, "Uncle! Where are you?"

Immediately Wodenstag and his brothers Donnerstag and Samstag ran to the edge of the river. They stared through the clear water. There was their Uncle Russel, his eyes wide open, a red cloud of blood issuing from his face

[Four]
Pertelote Sings a Compline,
and Chauntecleer a Matins

Chauntecleer stood on the shore of Wyrmesmere, that boundless southern sea. Behind him the earth-scar stretched from horizon to horizon, east and west and, as it seemed, circling half of the globe. Even in the night the earth-scar made itself known, for Chauntecleer had crossed it afoot, walking a dead land, flat and salted and silent.

As if in a dream the Rooster heard the cries and the dyings of his Animals. The battles returned to his memory. John Wesley was carrying the Wee Widow Mouse who was dead in his arms. The Stag Nimbus was sinking to his knees, his face lifted to the heavens, his grey tongue thrust out. And the reptilian Cockatrice was soaring over all..

Wyrmesmere. It was so called because Wyrm himself had formed its vastitude.

In front of the Rooster the moon laid low upon the waters, a pewter disk. From the moon to the Rooster's feet it sent a rippling path, an invitation to walk forward and to drown.

Chauntecleer said, "Lazara, come."

A small dark shadow came tweedling across the scar. Lazara the Black Beetle fetched up beside the Rooster and waited.

They knew each other, the Rooster and the Beetle, from disasters past, for it was Lazara that had buried the bodies of his three sons.

Chauntecleer said, "Follow me."

He strode to a particular place where once his battlement had been thrown up against the enemy. Lazara joined him there. He said, "Here, on this spot, dig the Fox's grave."

Lazara moved on her tweezer feet, assessing the soil. "We're near the sea," she said.

"This is where he fought. This is where he tore the Basilisks asunder. This is where I want him buried."

"Aye, sir. But the water makes a dreary grave. It'll scour the hole from below and could cause a fearful stink o' the bones and maybe send them topside again."

"Then dig to stone and keep the water out."

The Beetle, her whole head hidden in a black hood, sat still, considering. "Well," she said, "Could be a crypt could trick it."

"Dig one."

"Aye. 'Tis my profession and my skill, digging in any sorter substance as presents itself. I think I can piece it for you. Only—"

Chauntecleer jerked his head. "This is a dead land," he snapped. "Damnably crabbed and cold and dead. Find your stone, Black Lazara, and dig Lord Russel his crypt, and keep your 'onlys' for those who lack decision."

Then, without a glance at the Beetle, Chauntecleer took his solitary way back across the ruins of the earthwork. He passed the place where the Coop once stood.. A frigid wind blew off the sea, slipping through the Rooster's feathers, for there was no windbreak behind him nor a rustling of leaves in the forest ahead of him.

He paused and looked around. Under the dull moon Chauntecleer saw that all the leaves had been stripped away. The forest was naked. The weather had skipped a season. Too soon winter was upon them.

In her husband's absence Lady Pertelote sang a most merciful Compline.

> "Lullay-lulee, lulee-lulay,
> A sorrow hath borne our Lord away.
>
> It bore him up, it bore him down
> On wings as soft as eiderdown.
>
> It set him on an iron earth
> To fashion a deep sepulcher."

After midnight Chauntecleer returned. He stood a silent vigil beside the Fox's body.

Neither hearing him nor seeing him, Pertelote felt his presence below the boughs of the maple. She spread her wings and sailed the distance down, then settled close to her Rooster.

"The preparations are complete?" she said.

"They will be."

"Tomorrow," she said, "we will finish the business, my sisters and I. We will wash him and dress him for his eternity."

As if to himself alone, Chauntecleer murmured: "Wyrm for a day. Wyrm for a season. But who can endure him forever?"

The Hen and the Rooster then sat in a perfect silence.

Against the starry sky the farther trees were silhouettes, their arms and fingers skeletal.

A little sound stirred in the night: "Hooo, hooo."

Pertelote whispered, "The Mice are crying."

Chauntecleer said, "Comort them."

She did. She walked to a hole in the ground.

"Samstag," she said, "is that you?" "Well, it's me."

"Are you awake, then?"

"Hooo, hooo."

"Is it a dream that saddens you?"

"Yes," said the Mouse. "No."

"Do you mind if I sit here a while?"

"It is a kindness, Lady."

A second voice spoke: "But we are all awake."

"Ah, Wodenstag."

"Maybe," said Wodenstag. "Could you maybe hold us?"

"I could," said Pertelote.

All the Brothers Mice crept out of their hole and tucked themselves under the Hen's breast.

Not far away an itchy voice said, "There has been none of us asleep this night." Tick-Tock the Black Ant.

Chauntecleer stood up. He took to the air and circled to the crown of the maple. and crowed a Matins of nearly unbearable tenderness. He was rigid, to be sure—but as a tuning fork is rigid. He shed a music so penetrating that the very core of the Animals' uncertainty was stung to sweetness.

Ah, the skill of Chauntecleer! He sang the Fox's name. He included the dead in this common litany. But Russel's death-night had *become* the night, and death too was rendered common, ah. He enfolded even the dead into the hearts of the Hens, and they mourned their brother freely. Mourning was given a voice, easy words, old familiar words. Matins was that voice, and the impacted pressure of the Animals' souls found release. They wept.

Pertelote's eyes too went warm and damp. But her tears

were for the thing that she was hearing: the extraordinary priesthood of Lord Chauntecleer. And for this too: that in her husband there was not a scrap of relief.

[Five]
In Which Russel is Laid to Rest

The Animals filed south from the maple tree.

Tick-Tock the Black Ant led his troops in the vanguard, a military parade to honor Lord Russel the Fox of Good Sense, troops like a carpet cleansing the route for the funeral procession behind.

Ten Hens did duty as pallbearers, four to one side, four to the other, and two to carry Russel's bushy tail. His corpse was heartbreakingly light, the sickness having wasted him to fur and bones. He was covered in a mantle woven of breast feathers, and the mantle had been sweetened by the Queen of the Honey Bees and by her Family Swarm. Behind the Hens came Pertelote, singing verses as she went. And then the Mice. And John Wesley, frowning mightily and stepping wayward, as though he had nothing to do with funerals.

Over the entire procession flew Chauntecleer. The sun made him magnificent: his coral comb like the crenels of a castle wall; his feathers proudly golden, his beak black, his nails white, his legs azure, his flight commanding, his manner unapproachable.

Perhaps the Animals were going to bury war forever. No.

The Keepers of universal Evil can never retire into a quiet insignificance. The good order of the whole creation requires their labors, and what they are gives heaven pause.

A funeral? A small communal ceremony? Yes, of course, but so much more. It was a quasar, a deep and soundless pulse in space, a signal of the end and of a beginning.

Let no one wonder, then, that Wyrm himself saw fit to attend this funeral. His future stratagems demanded it.

Lazara the Beetle met this procession on the near edge of the earth scar. Chauntecleer alighted beside her. To him her lumpish crouch seemed premonitory, and her blackness forbidding. Therefore he flew forward alone.

He spoke to her in private tones. "There'd better be a reason why you're waiting here, Beadle Lazara. I told you where to dig the grave."

"Aye," said Lazara. "But … come and see."

She led the Rooster toward an obvious hole and beside the hole a mound of stone-chips heaped up.

"I've digged you a crypt, but…"

"But *what?*"

"Oh, sir, I digged it in solid stone, and no crack nor fissure in it. I swear it as a surety. But…" She cowled her face.

Chauntecleer was on the verge of a crow. "*Out* with it!"

"How it chanced, I don't know. I cannot say. Sir Chauntecleer, there's a treachery in its bottom."

Chauntecleer strode ahead of the Beetle. At the crypt he was hit by an odor of stinking corruption. His eyes burned. Yet he peered over the edge. As Lazara had said, the sepulcher was well scooped, the sides of it carved and smooth. But on its floor lay a long extrusion, a thick ooze slick and passive.

The Rooster hissed, "A turd! Lazara! Who would shit in Russel's grave?"

"Oh, no! No, sir!" The Beetle seemed unaffected by the stench. "'Tis a living thing. Come of its own self-choosing."

Chauntecleer turned his face toward the sea. "Wyrmesmere!"

"Well, I don't know nothing of this Wyrmes-whatchoo-call-it, no I don't. Only just, I looked and the thing was there."

The Rooster crowed a crow so angry that the whole procession went stark still.

Braving the stench, Chauntecleer leaped in Russel's crypt, clawed the loathsome coil, and with his beak scissored it into two parts. Then he rose from the hole bearing the pieces in his talons, and pitched them into the endless sea.

"This is *my* doing! Wretched Wyrm—*choke* on your works!"

If such a thing is possible, the waves smiled to receive the divided slug.

"There will be a grave!" Chauntecleer shouted. "And it shall *not* be defiled!"

He called the Queen of the Family Swarm and commanded that she and her Bees line the sepulcher with an impermeable wax, and then to sweeten the wax with a honey as with myrrh. Even so the Rooster sanctified the tomb

When the grave was cleansed and waxed, Lord Chauntecleer scattered his own golden feathers as a bed for Russel. Then he stood back and held himself in royal self control.

"It is done," he said. "Bring my brother. Lay him to his rest."

And so they did.

Gently the wings of ten Hens lowered the Fox, quiet under his shroud and featureless, except for his red tail whose tip was inked in black.

The Mice selected stone shavings the size of their hands

and dropped them like pebbles upon their uncle. "Earth to earth." Tick-Tock said to his troops. With sand and stone-dust the Ants covered the corpse. Pertelote sang an elegy, to which the Animals sang a choral refrain.

And in the end, Chauntecleer did his part. As was proper at eventide, he sang:

> "Guide us waking, O Lord,
> And guard us sleeping.
> That awake we may watch with thee,
> And asleep we may rest in peace."

PART TWO

In Fimbul-Winter

[Six]
In which Rachel Coyote Discombobulates her Husband

In the great northern forests, crouched on a carpet of brown needles under a canopy of tall pine trees, a Coyote is hiding. His forelegs are low, his butt high behind, and his narrow snout seeming to grin with all of his teeth.

Well: *thinks* he is hiding.

In fact, his skinny, rust-red self is in full view. But this is the way the Coyote hides: he freezes. Poor Ferric, convinced that perfect stillness effects perfect invisibility. But he isn't grinning. He's scared. His cheeks go back to his ears, and his eyes narrow into two darts whose points point to the bridge of his muzzle. Fear turns Ferric Coyote into one long, taut nerve, like an arrow fixed mid-flight, or a bowstring which, if it is touched, would hum at a high pitch: *Eeeeeeee!*

Ferric has frozen this way often in his lifetime, ever since life itself became for him a dangerous proposition. The Coyote is cursed with senses too keen for a fainting heart; or, *volte-face,* keen senses have caused his heart to faint.

His ears are dishes; they hear everything. The pads of his

paws are raw, and his bones are hollow tubes, and his skin is tympanic; they feel everything, and everything is magnified. He eyes are perpetually frightened; they see the least twitch in nature, for any twitch may be malicious, for there is no twitch he knows that doth love him.

Except for Rachel. She loves him. But the woman is inexplicable.

Lately the dangers have multiplied tenfold, and he's begun to ache with hiding. This is because of his wife, whom he loves in return, but who has *no* fears whatsoever—none. So Ferric yelps often and hides for two. And, the worser of worst, three weeks ago his wife took a notion to travel.

All at once summer was winter. All at once the land and the forests were locked hard against his busiest scratching. At the time Ferric thought that this was the reason why she began to trot away and away from their home into alien territories. But she wasn't seeking the heat of the south. Happy as a Plover (who, incidentally, were gone after warmer climes) Rachel has for twenty-one days been cantering *north!*—while he's been skittering and dashing and creeping and freezing and dashing again after her. Nor has he the slightest idea where they are going, or when they will get there.

"Rachel, where?"

"I'll know it when I see it." Careless. A woman without a care in the world. "And you will know it," she says, "when I tell you."

"For God's sake, Rachel, *when?*"

"When you're able," she says, and she laughs, and she goes.

Wel, Ferric can't allow her to travel the world undefended. Therefore—*zoooom*—he shoots ahead to scan the forests for disasters and to save her life, to freeze for two.

"Rachel! *Why?*"

"Oh, you'll see. Soon you will see."

Poor, poor Ferric. His speed has not rewarded him. For suddenly he finds himself crouch before the most perilous sight he has ever seen, and he is paralyzed in a freeze of spectacular petrification. He never imagined that such scenes could exist. And he almost bolted into it, but was saved at the last instant by instinct, quickness, and a skidding stop.

Ferric Coyote has come to the end of the forest.

Ferric Coyote is staring at open spaces!

There are no trees on all the vast land before him. Sweeps of frozen muskeg, low hillocks, stunted spruce, bald and blown stones, and sky, and sky, and sky, and—nothing! Infinity! Why, one more step and he would have exploded. The Creature who ventures into such an immensity would feel stark naked.

Ferric behind a stunted pine; Ferric, frozen beyond his capacities; Ferric cannot control his gullet. He swallows and swallows at the sight.

Then comes Rachel, and Ferric's heart fails.

Does she fear the diabolical fraud that nature has played by coming to an end? And is she duly buffaloed? No! No, no, no, *no!*

That woman! That red, relaxed, and reckless woman! When she draws close beside him, she looks out beyond the trees, and nods, and smiles, and murmurs, "Lovely."

He says the only thing he *can* say in his freeze: *"Tssssst!"*

She kisses his wooden jaw and trots straight out and onto the unholy blank.

He huffs. He puffs. He hyperventilates. And through his toothy grin he produces a steam of extreme alarm. Ferric is a petcock:

"Tsssssssssssst!"

Rachel hears and recognizes the intensity of Ferric's

sibilance, if not the sense of it. She looks back. Gently she returns to her husband, all her joints loose and her expression content. She nuzzles him—and he as sharp as a drawn arrow.

"Be at peace," she says. "Where we are, Ferric, is right and proper. Give me a little while to look—"

"*Tssst!*"

"—and I'll be back, and then what? Then I will tell you the good thing soon to happen for us."

Off again, with her fine bushy tail, as healthy as Ferric is horrified, Rachel trots sixty yards away, one hundred yards across the faceless landscape—and vanishes.

Ferric blinks. His hairs stand up. A rash of needles prickle his face.

"Rachel?"

Ferric is on his feet.

"Rachel!"

The Coyote gathers his strength and springs. He runs dead-level over the ground.

"*Rachel!*"

Then, as smoothly as she disappeared, she reappears, head, breast, and legs above the ground. And what is that? She… Rachel is laughing.

So Ferric drives his forelegs to a stop. He executes a quick turn and dashes back into the forest.

"Oh, Ferric, Ferric," the woman exults. "Can you believe our good fortune? I have found it!"

What Ferric has, he has a headache. He has a wife.

Rachel is breathless. So is he. But hers is merriment, and his is terror. His wife doubles back and finds him hiding. She puts a paw to his ribs and tickles him. He will not be tickled.

"Oh, be at peace," she laughs. "I have found the perfect den."

"Hmph, woman. Hmph."

"It's warm. Steam comes out through cracks in the stones below. Isn't that wonderful? It is exactly what I hoped for. It's why we've come."

"Good," mutters Ferric. "Let's go back."

"Back? Oh, Ferric."

Rachel nuzzles him. "No, not back," she says full kindly. "The whole purpose is, we've come to stay."

It is at this point that the Coyote's eyes water, and he starts to mew in his throat.

"Shhh, my dear, brave husband. What I've been looking for is a home is a home for a home for our family."

"Family? Rachel, did you say *family?*"

"You," she says—and he notices a sheen of tears in her eyes. "You and me and our babies. I am soon to bear a batch of little Coyotes."

[Seven]
The Mighty Hemlock Tree

The world skipped autumn and winter clicked it cold. The grass in the fields withered, yellow and sere. Roses were blasted on the bush, and its soft stems turned brittle. Touch them and they cracked. The wind that blew in from the sea produced an evening fog.

It was in a thick twilight fog that Chauntecleer heard a wheezy word arise from the ground: "Willows" was the word. "Willows."

The Rooster lowered his head and cocked one eye and saw a solitary Woolly Worm making slow haste to parts unknown. Her coat—rings of burnt umber and sienna—was as dense as Sheep's wool.

"Willows," the worm wheezed. "The willows are froze, and where will I find a tender one now?"

Chauntecleer said, "Pardon me, grandmother. I couldn't help but overhear—"

Though it was hard to tell, given her slowth, the Woolly Worm stopped. "Bless me," she said. "The fog talks."

"No, ma'am. I'm Lord Chauntecleer. It's Rooster talking."

"Never did hear of a Lord Chauntecleer."

This set the Rooster back a bit. "Well," he said. He would have drawn himself up to his full dignity, except that the mists would have rendered dignity invisible. "Well, it's time you met a Chauntecleer. I am he."

She said, "No force to it, nor no thrill to me." Then she continued her slow-motion crawl. The imperturbable Wooly Worm.

"What," said Chauntecleer, "is your intention, crossing my land? Where do you think you're going?"

"From winter. Into winter."

"Aye, winter indeed," he said. "But what's this about willows?"

"Willows are eatables," she said. "Eatables and sleepables, and here am I, caught in the cold unhoused."

The Rooster kept his eye an inch above the bunching unbunching, bunching unbunching woman. "You ask me," he said, "you're going in the wrong direction. There are willows clustered along the Liver-brook, but the Liver-brook's back the way your came."

"And haven't I been there? And isn't your brook frozen at the edges?"

"Already?"

"Already. Take me as a sign, laddy. In all my days I've never grown so thick a coat. It's a winter of rack and ruin upon us now. It's a winter as never was. To put a name to it,i t's Fimbul-winter that's come to kill."

Chauntecleer considered the matter. Actually, there was no reason not to believe the Wooly Worm. Woolly Worms predict winters. But this was a winter he'd never heard of before.

So he aimed his Rooster-eye ather and said, "Grandmother, Fimbul-winter?"

She answered, "A winter as might never know an ending.

And a winter that doesn't end, that puts paid to everything. Best you take my meaning, lad, before the time runs out."

The Worm's apprehensions troubled Chauntecleer, and the fog began to feel unfriendly. He said, "Be plain, grandmother. What is your meaning?"

"Prepare," she said. "Prepare."

And, *Prepare, prepare*, he heard from a dozen wheezings left and right of him.

The Rooster nosed out these other voices and found a host of Wooly Worms, each as deeply furred as the first, and all of them crawling in leaden haste, and every voice premonitory:

Prepare!

And so it was that when the fog burned off the following morning, Lord Chauntecleer spread his golden wings and sailed in circles crowing his Animals into service.

There was a sun in the cold sky, and there was the bright golden Rooster.

He made a trumpet of his voice. "All of you, the Creatures who can, gather foods of every kind!"

Pertelote said to Chauntecleer, "When we lose a landed place, my Lord, we must create a spiritual place in which to live." And she said, "Walls for tender hearts, a roof to enclose their spirits, a habitation in which the company of the Meek can lie down and survive hard times."

So Chauntecleer took to his wings and sailed high above the earth in order to find a winter home for the Animals and for their harvest.

He scanned the standing trees, the clearings, the brambles, the meadows, the upland ridges. He had a gift, did Chauntecleer. Though his eyes were not slanted like the Hawk's eyes, but as round as dimes, his daytime sight was keen.

An oily fog began to sweep the terrain below, concealing the small things and then the large. Finally one tree rose like a steeple out of the mists. Chauntecleer aimed his flight thither. A Hemlock, it was, its evergreen boughs furling itself like a robe.

Chauntecleer spiraled down the Hemlock—down and down the widening branches which cloaked a trunk as tall as a mast.

He landed. So wide was the tree's circumference that it surely embraced a space as large as a rotunda. He walked inside and found himself in something like a castle hall. Here the fog was banished. The wind was shut out. The earth was soft. A natural warmth caused the cold in him to shudder. And the undersides of the needles glimmered silver.

Here was a home. Here was space to larder a winter's full of foodstuffs. To this place Chauntecleer called the Animals.

The Mad House of Otter showed up without stopping to beg entrance. Slippery-sloppery, they scrambled in with caches of dried crustaceans, then they played and played, untroubled by Fimbul-winter. Whenever the notion took them, they humped through the woods until they found a fine, smooth slope. At the top of it they leaped, made streamlines of their bodies by folding their forelegs close to their chests, and tobogganed down at squint-eyed speeds.

Tick-Tock commanded one of his divisions to forage seeds with which to larder their underground chambers: wheatseeds, weedseeds, barleycorns, and oats. Another division of Ants gathered in baskets the last crystals of honeydew. Busy, busy, busily obedient, they marched in narrow pathways to and fro.

Busyness and work, sir; never shall we shirk, sir!

John Wesley Weasel stripped bark from the bases of trees:

spruce, cedar, black cherry, birch.

Everyone scattered and gathered. Chestnuts, hickory nuts, chestnuts, beechnuts, walnuts, acorns, gumballs spiked and most unsavory, and the poor kernel of the sycamore. They harvested the meat of collapsing gourds, the rinds of squashes, turnips, beets, the blasted crabapple, the woody pear, cabbage hearts, the sweet fiber of young saplings.

The Queen Honeybee and her Family Swarm could no longer find pollen in the blossoms that had let down their hair. But they could, and they did, protect the honey they'd already manufactured in their hives. They stored their sweet-stuffs deeply against the winter.

So did the Mice dart here and there, finding the vinegar pulp of fallen apples.

Five Hens scratched more furiously than ever before. Pertelote taught the other five (save fat Jasper) to dig roots where the frost allowed it, to collect bulbs and fungi and lichens and mosses, as well as the leaves and the grasses of healing herbs.

Sheep arrived and sheared the frosted vegetation close to the ground. Better than these nibbled bits, they bore with them a wool to warm a shivering Creature.

In the end Chauntecleer had administered an effective unity of purpose, foodstuffs not for gluttony but for saving against Fimbul-winter.

[Eight]
In Which Wyrm
Initiates His Stratagem

Wyrm's gross body clogs the caves through all the expanses under the mantle of the earth. His tail from the southern sea to the northernmost pole. He lies beneath the feet of the Animals, those whom Chauntecleer rules and those who wander the forests and the plains and the arctic tundra.

It was a piece of Wyrm that had extruded itself into Russel's crypt.

Now then. There lives on the marshy tussocks north of the boreal forests a Plain Brown Bird. As she considers it, she is of no account. Thus have the other Birds judged her, and she has never found an argument to counter them.

At the crack of the early winter, all the other Birds hurried their migrations. They took to the air, Geese thrusting their long necks forward and forming gracious V's to the south. Flocks of lesser Birds flew up in shapes of revolving clouds. The clouds stretched and broke and hastened south. Terns and

Plovers and a hundred varieties of loveliness all left the Plain Brown Bird behind unaccompanied, for she has always been crippled by timidity. Least is her name, though no one has ever asked it of her.

She flies on blunt wings, trimming her flight with an attenuated tail. She's dressed in drab. And wisdom has taught her not to bewail her state, but to accept it. Least is reconciled. She will be a spinster till the end.

Presently she finds a meager nourishment by piercing the frosty sedges with a long, narrow bill. This is her single tool, slightly curved and needle-sharp.

And then today—pleasure upon impossible pleasure— the plain brown Bird begins to hear a music. She twitches into the air to find the source of the music. It is a melody that tugs at her heart.

She should refuse it. Tenderness is nothing she deserves. But a yearning makes her break her rules.

She flies the tundra, following the sound.

It ascends in a single, easeful voice, a cordial song that seems to give itself freely away, both to the earth and to the turning spheres—and to a misfitting Bird.

Least smiles. Airborne, she discovers a crack in the tundra, a rocky defile, and descends, and the music grows louder. When she alights on the edge of the crack she feels a warming steam arising, comforting her.

Then the melody turns into words, and the words are love. It is a love song.

The words sing, "Plain" and "Brown" and "Oh, so lonesome" and "Come."

The words strike her heart and she tingles with fear and with desire.

Immediately the Singer sings a gentle and personal

sentence: "I overcome fear."

If she could, Least would fly away. For she knows the truth. She cannot be the object of anyone's love.

But the beautiful voice sings, "I know your name. I will call you by your name."

No, the Plain Brown Bird does not fly away. In spite of herself, she bows and listens like a communicant.

"The lady is Least. Come, my dearest Least, and I will make you mine."

The plain brown Bird realizes that she is crying.

"Nor," the Singer modulates his melody until it is a silken thread. "Nor is it too much to say that I love you."

He lies! Who can love a flaw in the handiwork of God? Least covers her face in the feathers of one blunt wing. Even in her disbelief she yearns to believe.

"Come and love me in return. It isn't loveliness I love. I love the heart deep within its plain brown dress."

Least murmurs, "Who are you?"

"Come and I will ask nothing—except a kiss. What is a kiss? The pressure of your marvelous bill. Give it away, and you have lost nothing. Give it to me, and the touch alone will make my beloved lovely."

Spinster Bird. Drab and dull, poor spinster Bird, she releases herself to the song. She spreads her blunt wings and floats into the hole.

"Ahhhh," the Singer sings, "she comes."

Least descends to the stones that lie at the bottom of the defile, then enters a cleft from which the ardent heat arises. Least is beyond decisions. She is beyond thought. It is her soul that answers. Below the stones a tunnel opens. Least flies the tunnel, unafraid of the darkness that surrounds her now.

The Singer sings a history of suffered injustices, of bitter and undeserved assaults, all of them borne courageously, sings of personal exile—and hasn't she known exile too? She has. Least nearly bursts with pity and with solace for the one who woos her.

The song lays down the trail before her. She plumbs the depths until the voice of the Singer is immediately before her and she can feel a presence as huge as a mountain underground. Least seems to be standing inside a cathedral hallway.

The voice changes into many voices, a demanding hiss of a thousand voices. No, this isn't lovely any more. It is not love.

"And now," the urgent chorus commands "the kiss!"

The Plain Brown Bird is, in fact, inside the Serpent's empty eye socket

A loud, drum-booming rhythm lifts her, carries her to the thin bone at the back of the socket.

"The Kiss!"

Least is no longer in control. She lost autonomy when her heart insisted *Follow.*

"Sum Wyrm sub terra," the Serpent sighs. "Kiss me and set me free."

A great force swells behind her. It drives her like a spear through the thin bone at the back of Wyrm's eye socket, drives her until her sharp bill plunges into the mud of his brain. Corruption and gore explode backward, sending the Plain Brown Bird out of the socket like a feather on a fountain. A hard gush of blood carries her up the long tunnel and all the way to the stones at the bottom of the earth-crack. And the blood, it sighs, "Thy kissing hath killed me. All is well."

Least's feathers are soaked. Her throat burns. She coughs, wretches, then vomits and vomits. Her bones shiver. She wishes she were dead.

When she tries to speak, the plain brown Bird discovers

that she has lost her voice.

One more calamity awaits her. In the weeks to come two Coyotes will begin to make a den on a shelf below the lip of the earth-crack. What will be left in Least to meet this new challenge? However will she be able to save them from the hell below?

[Nine]
In Which the Mr. and Mrs. Pertinax Cobbs Appear

Chauntecleer had chosen a residence more elegant than the Animals could ever have imagined. Instead of a ceiling, the interior space of the Hemlock soared up to the apex of a king's high tower.

Outside and inside and sashaying round and round their grand spaces, the Hens elevated their beaks to the angles of hauteur. Oh, how they gussied about like ladies of a royal pedigree, and each chose for herself a roosting branch as accomodating as the beds of princesses.

As far as the Mice were concerned, the great hall granted them a skedaddling land as wide as all outdoors. Then, when skedaddling gave way to the need for sizzle-snoring sleep, the good earth mothered them in a fine, small pocket for a nest.

The Family Swarm of Honey Bees left the old hives and fashioned new ones in the crotches of the Hemlock's sturdy limbs.

The Black Ants then engineered ground tunnels and bins wherein to store the winter's provisions.

Sheep lay themselves down outside the rim of the mighty Hemlock.

Somewhere in the tree's interior a Squirrel had built his nest of twigs and leaves. He skittered down the trunk to watch this new action below, then skittered up the trunk to frown in gloomy mediations. He thought he'd run unseen. In fact, the Weasel had heard the Squirrel's nails scratching bark, which got his back up. He told Chauntecleer that there was a bandit above them. Chauntecleer flew through the limbs of the Hemlock until he found the nest.

"Who," he said, "are you?"

"Who," the Squirrel answered, "are *you?*"

"Chauntecleer, captain and commander."

"Chauntecleer, land-thief and plunderer. I was here first."

"And you can surely stay. There's room enough here for herds and oxen, flocks and belly-crawlers."

"Me, I take up a whole tree. I need room!"

"You!" the Rooster crowed, "won't have a butt to sit on once I chew it to pulp. What is your name?"

A Rooster is five times the size of a Squirrel. Grudgingly this Squirrel answered, "Ratotosk the Grey Squirrel."

And so it was that the Society of Animals felt themselves well settled and protected.

Nation shall not lift up swords against nation,

Neither shall they learn war any more.

Pertinax the Ground Squirrel had not complained when a clutch of babbling Hens began to trample and scratch the soil above his burrow; had not complained when they busified the daylight with perpetual peckings and scratchings. Neither had he complained when Sheep of a noxious stink and squadrons of Insects bleated and buzzed and broke his sleep in his nest among the roots of the World-Tree which his family had inhabited for generations and generation past.

But now he stood erect on the mound beside his doorway, watching with dismay the bustle of immigrants, and realizing that they planned to make their homes above his own.

So sure was he of his not-complaining that he had freely, nay, *fearlessly* put the question to his wife.

Down into his passages he went, and into the bedroom where Mrs. Cobb was weaving a pallet for their long nap. "Mrs. Cobb," he said, "you decide. Am I complaining?"

"Why, no, Mr. Cobb."

"Right!" he said, and straightway raced up a passage to the heap of his residue dirt, where he sat and held his narrow body erect, having been assured that he was indeed a tolerant Ground Squirrel and a not-minding-the-new-neighbors neighbor—though he *did* put a rather more severe twitch to his whiskers.

Neither had Pertinax Cobb minded the proudful presence of that golden Rooster, nor the metronomic regularity of his crowing, for he valued schedules and disciplines. Besides, the tender mercies of the Bird's midnight Matins always sent his wife into a puppyhood of peaceful dreamings.

What Pertinax *did* mind, when all at once the winter had slammed the land, was that now he could *not* go to sleep!

Pertinax the Ground Squirrel had been planning on that sleep. It was the tradition of Ground Squirrels everywhere to sink into a three-months' slumber, which was their pleasant reward for the three months of their hard labor preparing for the frigid season. Indeed: before this migrant population arrived, Pertinax had dashed abroad, stuffing harvests into his cheek's pouches until they bulged with prosperity, and then, back in his tunnels, pouring the foodstuffs into granaries. Moreover—

before this ruck-ruckering ruckus—he had concentrated on the seeds that he and Mrs. Cobb loved the most: the winged seeds from the fallen cones of the Hemlock Tree.

"Mrs. Cobb, Mrs. Cobb!"

It was midnight. The Ground Squirrel poked his wife awake.

"What is it, Mr. Cobb?"

"Did you hear that?"

"Hear what, Mr. Cobb?"

"Did you feel that?"

"Feel what, Mr. Cobb?"

"I think the earth quaked."

"In fact," Mrs. Cobb answered, "I dreamed of a bumping and a sprinkling of dust."

"There! That's what I'm talking about."

"It wasn't a dream?"

"I don't want to complain."

"You are a wonderful not-complainer."

"But I can't sleep."

"Mr. Cobb, I am sorry for you."

"*You* sleep."

"That too. I am sorry for that too."

"I think some somebody just chopped off a limb of the tree."

"My, but that is very disconcerting."

"A limb, Mrs. Cobb. A very big limb—of the Hemlock!"

"I don't doubt it. Nobody puzzles puzzles better than you, Mr. Cobb."

"I am at the end of my rope. If they break our tree, what then? They break our *world.*"

"Well, Mr. Cobb, I believe the time has come."

"The time has come indeed."

So Pertinax Cobb the Ground Squirrel betook himself to the door of his personal burrow, and hopped up onto his mound, and straightened his spine in order to complain from the highest of his height, and chittered furiously. If he couldn't sleep, no one should sleep. If they disrespected the Hemlock, they must depart the Hemlock. One Creature—it was the Rooster, by the hearing of it—went flapping off into the night.

But no one else stirred. Snozzle-snorings from the Mice's pocket-pouch. Sleep-clucks from the branches, and antennae-tickings from countless Instects under the ground. But not a single cackle of fear.

No one seemed to notice the Ground Squirrel's scoldings. Except Mrs. Cobb, who loved him.

Pertelote was awake. She too had felt the earth tremor. And then, by the sudden coolness at her right wing, she felt the absence of Lord Chauntecleer.

The first had wakened her. The second caused her soul a quick disquietude, because her husband had said "Wyrm" with his old bitterness, and his flight had been angry.

A half hour later she heard someone muttering at the roots of the tree.

"By-cause Chickies sneaked away! John knows! Didn't his burrow bust and tumble down on him? Didn't a *Boom* bury him? And he to grub him poor self out or *die*? And what when he come up? Wasn't nobodies what told John Double-U, 'Come out, come out, and run away.' Nor nobodies what said, 'Bye-bye.' Nor not neither a 'Stick-it-in-your-ear.'"

Pertelote heard the Weasel scratch around the trunk of the tree, forth and back, seeking something.

"John, he smells gone-ness. And the only somebody in sight is John!"

Pertelote heard distinctly a Weasel-nose scrape against a tree root.

"Gaw!"

A Mouse said, "Step-papa? Is that you?"

There came a grunt, then a shuffling, and then a bark, "Mices! Move over!"

Three of the Brothers Mice said, "Hello, Step-papa."

The first Mouse spoke through a yawn: "Good night."

And a Weasel said, "Ack."

It was during that same night that Fimbul-winter with a might slam concluded all seasons except itself. If the moon was cold, earth was colder. The fog snapped and became crystals of ice. Ice whitened the ground, creating a pale light. The clouds swept in and cloaked the universe.

[Ten]
In Which the Dun Cow
Makes Herself Known

Sing, says a voice.

And a voice says, *What shall we sing?*

A voice says, *Sing of heroes and their witnesses.*

The voice of a thousand congregations seethes: *Arma virumque.*

Chauntecleer stands beside Russel's grave. In dark night he had flown here. In darkness he stands, listening. The words he hears come hissing from the surface waters of Wyrmesmere. And he can *see* them, for they arise as a kind of ghostly light, an *ignis fatuus* that he can see slant, but cannot see by on.

It was the slumping of the earth that drew him thither. He feared he's find Russel's sepulchar broken open and his bones dishonored. But the tomb was still intact. Then the sea has destroyed the Rooster's relief—by speaking.

Sing.

What shall we sing?

Sing encomia.

How meet, right, and salutary it is to praise the great now gone before us.

Fimbul-winter has forged the Liverbrook into a winding snake of ice, its mouth a paralyzed bite at the coast of Wyrmesmere. Lakes and rivers; what once were the autumnal roaring foam and the quiet pools; the rills and ponds and fountains and the mighty mountain falls—all these are fixed in dream-shapes, anvils and unbreakable spears.

The air in this place is stinks of salt

Sing.

What shall we sing?

Praise Russel the Fox. Glorify his memory. For he took Vipers in his mouth and died that others might live.

Yes: in his soul Chauntecleer too praises the Fox. Russel did not scorn his duty. He deserved his feathered bier and the devout "Amen" of the whole community. Chauntecleer cannot gainsay the sea's homage. But it pinions him nonetheless.

Sing of him, the Anointed, who by vast love and a hornèd spear....

Mundo Cani Dog! Chauntecleer resists the memory. He would leave if he were not spellbound. He covers his ears. But the words slide into his brains.

Sing of him who blinded monarchs. Apotheosize the Hound of the most stunning humility.

All at once, Chauntecleer is sobbing. Mundo Cani, who proved himself the paragon of warriors—he does. He deserves the greater homage.

The Rooster is staggered by the shame these words have renewed in his breast.

And now the voice grows thunderous, crashing like rolling breakers: *Sum Wyrm, ab Cane caecor!*

The Language of the powers! And Chauntecleer is struck dumb.

The light on the sea now glows like a field white with fire.

But then the next words flow over the Rooster's as a father warms his children in winter. They bring consolation.

Like woodwinds they sing, *But you, O Lord of the Coop that was, and of the Tower that is: your glory has never been extinguished. What is a Dog to the grandeur that shall be yours?*

Chauntecleer cocks his head sideways. With his left eye he peers at the gaseous light. Nor does he blink, lest he miss something of the future unrolling now before him.

Who is this that knows the work of Mundo Cani? Who is this that promises a heroism superior to the Dog's?

We sing of the penultimate hero. For there exists yet one heart able slay the horrors underground.

Chauantecleer is panting. Even so quickly have these sweet predictions cleansed his soul of regret, and then filled the space with hope. Lost in his desiring, he is unaware that the warmth of the sea has been blown away by a Fimbul-freeze.

One heart is shapen in nobility. One there is—for there is no one else on this round glob—who is worthy to be shown the navel to the netherworld.

Chauntecleer hears what is spoken of himself. Of himself! After even *Pertelote* had demanded penance for his transgressions. No, the Rooster will not question the singers' veracity. By wish and by want, he permits his own transfiguration.

The voices are French Horns. *You, Galle forte—you are the Chosen One. You alone can descend Wyrm's caverns and arise again triumphant.*

By his left eye Chauntecleer peers as far as sight allows him over the sea of his commissioning. He strains to see his benefactor. The singing seethes, and this is what he sees: the waves combusting into a dance of ghostly light. Upon the waves is the source of their combustion: a slick of oil. And a tarry scent reaches his nostrils, blown at him on a benumbing wind. The oil spreads and thickens, forming an island against whose edges the waves begin to lap.

It pleases Chauntecleer to be vouchsafed the birth of an island on which there is no snow, under which there is no ice. Wyrmesmere is proof against the winter.

He and the sea! What heart can*not* triumph in such a company?

A single voice now, formal in its declaration: *O brave Rooster, today have I made you my son.*

The pastel light diminishes, but Chauntecleer is not troubled. The icy breeze continues. His left eyeball has grown cold in its socket, and the more cold because the rest of his body burns with wild electricity.

The son of the sea.

The Rooster turns back toward the north. He moves without haste, glad for the solitude in which to savor his new station in life. If he isn't home by Lauds, well, then he isn't home by Lauds. He will choose to arrive when he will, for he comes with new purpose, and every Animal will exult in a Lord so bright with glory.

Suddenly, at some distance ahead of him, he spies another kind of light altogether, a spitting light, a narrow spouting of blue light.

Chauntecleer's hackles stand up and quiver the way they do before the rip-*crack!* of a lightning bolt.

He is unnerved.

Abruptly the point from which the sparks shoot is right beside him. The sparks project from something like a long spear. The spear swings low and touches his breast, and the Rooster gasps. This is no spear. It is the single horn of the Dun Cow.

"You are a dream!" he yells and casts his head to the side.

The Dun Cow says, "Look at me."

The scent of her breath is as sweet as timothy and a motherly as cud. Her voice is the low pipe of an organ.

"Look at me."

Chauntecleer, the baptized. Chauntecleer, grown bold by the sea's adoption, crows, "No!" He is, by God, better than the Dog!

Chauntecleer crows again, "You gave Mundo Cani more comfort than ever you gave me. No!"

"Chauntecleer, look at me."

"Shut up! Go away! I know you, woman. You say you suffer with suffering Creatures. You said you wanted to bear *my* suffering. You made a weakling of me. But I am not suffering now!"

The Rooster refuses to turn toward her, the witchery Cow, this wringer of souls.

In deep, lowing tones the Dun Cow says, "You are in harm's way, child. Lend me your fresh afflictions. Look at me."

After a moment the Dun Cow removes her sizzling horn from Chauntecleer. He is free to leave.

But in the night and in its silences she begins to sing an awe-ful song in long and lofty notes:

> "He who is ungrateful, he refuses me.
>> 'I will not look on thee.'
> And she, untroubled by his strife, replies,
>> 'Who made the eyes but I?'"

Chauntecleer fights to see before him what he sees inside his mind: her moist, resistless, long-lashed gaze.

She sings:

"'You must sit down,' says Love, 'and taste my meat.'
Come, child, sit and eat."

It is a beatitude, a palpable mercy. The Dun Cow stands unmoving. Waiting. Poor Chauntecleer is invaded by her compassion. She offers him no praise. Her promise is comfort, and in her presence even Fimbul-winter seems to release its grip.

"Humility, Chauntecleer. It is the beginning of wisdom."

In spite of himself the Rooster lifts his head. He turns ghis left eye to the Dun Cow, finally to look at in hers.

But he does not see her. He cannot see her! That eye is blind, frozen as hard as a marble.

The charm breaks. He had almost…. Chauntecleer had almost fallen for her blandishments. But what high irony! He was saved by his loss of sight.

Be gone, Cow!

The Rooster repents humility and swells again with glorious purpose.

PART THREE

John Wesley is in his Element Now

[Eleven]
In Which Three Pups are Named

Rachel is thirsty. It is a consuming thirst. Not that *she* is consumed by it, but that Ferric is. He worries, on account of, he is a Coyote and not a physician, and who is he to figure out the troubles in his dear wife's tummy?

But she *will* not stay protected in their den, and he *cannot* let her trot off on her own; therefore, they go together into the forest to find rivulets or streams or puddles. On this particular afternoon in the selfsame week after finding her den, Rachel is happily lapping fresh water with a blithe disregard of dangers. Ferric is hiding.

All at once a shifting deep underground and a quake on its surface cause both Coyotes to stumble and fall. Ferric's stiff bones nearly crack in half. His hissing comes so forcefully it bids fair to loosen a tooth or two.

Rachel herself is up on her feet and would continue drinking, except that, all in a flash, the stream freezes solid.

She looks at this wonderment and says, "Interesting."

Interesting! For his part, Ferric's sinews go so taut he

could skitter up tree trunks. And he would race to safety— but this earth-tremble like this one must have canceled safety everywhere.

Rachel says, "Well, there is one warm place." She canters north, out of the forest, across the iron-hard wilderness, and back to the den.

As she goes, Ferric shoots past her.

She is thinking about the heat of the steam that rises from the stones below their muskeg-hole. The den itself is a chamber at the end of a three-foot crawl-way, and is set about a foot below the tundra. At the opening of the crawl-way is a ledge wide enough to land four-footed on. The chamber large enough to accomodate two grown Coyotes and little pups, when the pups should come.

Rachel says, "Well, would you look at that."

For the steam produces a wandering cloud in the cold above their hole, an exhalation more voluminous than it was when they left this morning.

She jumps to the ledge and looks down and understands the reason for the greater heat. The stones at the bottom have moved, creating steps into a lower hole, a kind of tunnel that drops into blackness.

Ferric is back on the edge of the defile, squinting down. Rachel says, "Ferric? It's time," then retreats into the den's chamber.

"Time? Time?" He crouches on the tundra. The cold has crisped his whiskers. The pads of his paws are melting small depressions in the unaccountable ice.

Ferric Coyote thinks he hears sobbing in their den.

"Rachel?"

He pops his paws loose from the ice and drops onto the stony ledge. Yes! His wife is sobbing! She huffs between her sobs. She grunts pitifully on account of the pressure that pushes the sound out of her lungs.

"Rachel!"

The noises stop. For an instant Ferric is torn between freezing before the dangers in the den and rushing to his wife.

"Rachel, here I come."

"Ferric?"

"What?"

"It's time. But this is no time for you. Stay where you are."

"But—"

"You don't know now much I love you, Ferric. Let me love you from here."

So, then: he freezes again.

And it seems that Rachel is trying with all her might not to laugh.

Her grunting grows intolerable. Then she cries, "Whoop!" And she whispers, "Here's the first."

"Whoop!" she says. And, again, "Whoop!"

Now the woman is giggling. He hears a *Lick-licking* back inside the chamber.

After several wretched minutes, Rachel calls, "Come in, Ferric. Come meet my love for you."

Poor Ferric. Poor ignorant Coyote. He gets down on his elbows and his knees, hyperventilating himself dizzy, and crawls to his bumfuzzeling wife.

"Oh, my solemn husband, I have three gifts for you," she says at his approach. "And maybe you can laugh today."

In dim light Ferric makes out three glistering bundles. The bundles squeak. They wriggle. Rachel is lying on her side. He sees how big her nipples have grown. He sneezes, embarrassed by the sight of nipples. But look how the three bundles are squirming to Rachel's nipples. And biting them! Mauling them?

But Rachel sighs sweetly. She says, "This one is your son. These are your daughters. I will name the daughter-pups. You name our newborn boy."

Ferric Coyote thinks he is in pain. But the pain twists in him like pleasure. Such pleasure he has never known before. It brings tears to his eyes.

Children.

Compulsively, as though the name has always been waiting for its reason, Ferric whispers, "Benoni."

"Good," says Rachel. "A perfect name. And to our pretty little girls I give the names Twill and Hopsacking."

The other part of his pain is this: now Ferric Coyote must protect not one, but *four!*

Oh, the exhaustion of it all.

[Twelve]
In Which John Wesley Weasel Receives an Assignment

Because Chauntecleer had been absent the long night through, Pertelote prepared to crow Lauds in his place. Lovely Lady of the community, she could comfort the Animals. That was her gift. But she could not excite them to generous and purposeful labors. That was her husband's gift.

But just as the dark started to resolve itself into a grey dawn light, the duty was taken away from her. Chauntecleer stood on the crown of the Hemlock.

The first Canonical Crow of the morning streaked the low sky as if the sun had indeed arisen. Lauds seemed to strike heaven with vermillion spears: Lauds, as if the Rooster's mouth were the bell of a silver trumpet.

> "Blessèd be the Lord
> Who keeps his word;
> The Lord of Lights
> Who shall redeem your lives—"

Chauntecleer's Jovian paean roused the Animals to a

scarcely remembered wonder. Ears shot up. Eyes widened.
A small hole spat up seven Mice, one at a time. Pertinax,
unsleeping still, was transfigured. He raced the length of
his tunnel and popped up perpendicular at the doorway.
The passive Sheep slowly thought a thought. Someone was
declaring them worthy and their presence important.

> "O worship the great Creator
> Who sends a Savior
> To make your labors
> Holy."

There had been no Matins that night. Sleepers had
suffered deceitful dreams. They dreamed of banquets spread
before them, and of invitations to eat. They tried to eat, but
their stomachs cramped on hollow promises, and dinner
turned to dust in their mouths.

Oh, but what a Laud's! The Rooster's Crow seemed to
snatch back cloudy curtains to reveal a colorful stage and a
magical entertainment for the delight of all the Creatures in
Lord Chauntecleer's care.

> "And I, by the Lord God's choice,
> Shall be the voice
> That bids you eat
> The feast in peace!"

Pertelote stepped from the thatched Hemlock into the
waking day. She lifted her eyes and gazed at her husband
perched on the highest spire, Chauntecleer, so golden and so
coral-crowned.

Except that this winter was a Fimbul-winter, he should
have banished the fog and the foul air.

The Rooster was radiant, his jet-black beak, his stockings

dipped in the purple dyes of nobility.

When Lord Chauntecleer had brought Lauds to its last silvery notes, he sailed down and turned to the tasks of the day.

Skinny Chalcedony was already at work on the frozen ground outside the Hemlock tower. She was scratching at the glassy ice under which a cone was visible. Its scales were open, its small wing-seeds exposed. She scratched and scratched at the ice until it was laced with blood.

Chauntecleer stood beside her.

"Chalcedony."

The Hen snapped upright, glanced at him, then swiftly bowed her head.

"The Lord Rooster," she murmured, "dasn't spend breath on this tag of a barren, unpretty Hen."

But with his beak Chauntecleer jackhammered the ice until he'd broken through and Chalcedony's seeds were free.

The tasks of the day: he became the assessor of bins, of storage rooms, and of all the foodstuffs stockpiled against the sub-zero winter. The Animals had gathered a bountiful harvest.

Here, then, was the salvation of every Creature that otherwise would starve on the iron, unforthcoming earth. And he alone, Chauntecleer himself, had been appointed their Savior, the Lord of the populations whose homes were spread even unto the ends of the earth—for hadn't the sea told him so?

"John Wesley Weasel," Chauntecleer called, "I have an assignment for you!"

He heard a snort inside the Hemlock hall.

On splendid wings the Rooster flew through the boughs and straight to the Mouse-nest. He poked his beak inside and said, "It's a vocation, John. No one but you can do this thing."

This time there came no snort.

"Come, my little Buster, and go. Run through the forests. Run through the fields and the valleys and all the wilds, persuading Animals find food in this place,."

"It's a John Double-u the Rooster wants?"

Chauntecleer withdrew his beak. "No one *but* a Weasel," he announced. Then he called to all the Animals, "Which one of you has the gumption to brave strange lands and bring the hungry ones in?"

A vast silence followed his call.

John Wesley said, "Is a Double-u, right? Chickies and nobodies else, right?"

"Right!"

And so it was that John Wesley Weasel laid aside his gloom and jumped into the light and plumped his fur and said, "Is a John Double-u what's got scars of mighty battles. Is a John what's gave up his ear to win wars."

"And no he is a Weasel of independence and admirable fortitude. Are you ready, John?"

"Hoopla! John, he's *ever* ready!"

Chauntecleer, proud of his own providence, watched the Weasel shoot out of the Hemlock hall. At the same time he noticed a flash of white outside. His Pertelote.

He went to her.

"What medicinals, Lady?" he asked. "Balms? Lotions? Can you heal the famished when they come?"

"Everyone who comes."

Chauntecleer smiled and kissed the fire-red feathers at her throat. He felt a shiver pass through her body. "For thou art beautiful, my love," he murmured.

And she murmured in return, "He peeled a straw, a summer's thistle...."

"Just so," he said, then he raised his coral-red comb, the

banner of the undefeated, and turned and took to his wings.

So quickly had the Rooster begun to solve the starvations not only of his Animals, but of all the families under heaven, that Pertelote felt an adoration greater than when she first met the him and gave herself to him in marriage.

But at his turning she gasped.

In spite of his radiance and his lordly confidence, her husband was not whole. If he had waited, she would have begged an explanation. His left eyeball revolved in its socket a solid, pale-blue orb.

As for the rest of Chauntecleer's community, at the end of this wonderful day they went cheerfully to their beds and fell into dreamless, peaceful sleeps.

Alleluia! The golden Commander had crowed the duties of the daylight hours with such assurance and with such good order that no one could not *not* labor, nor anyone neglect the needs of the others.

"Pertinax Cobb," Chautecleer had called, and the Ground Squirrel, stunned that the Rooster knew his name, popped up from his hnole.

The Rooster had said, "I know the ways of the frugal. They fill their warehouses with food enough to outlast the winter season." He'd swept one wing wide, gesturing to the Creatures busy around the Hemlock. "Behold your brothers and your sisters. They are here to serve you as much as you serve them."

Mrs. Cobb came and sat beside her husband, her quartermaster Mr. Cobb.

The Rooster said to both of his whole community, "Serve each other as faithfully as kith serves kin."

Pertelote spent that night roosting on the limb she shared with Chauntecleer, though once again the Rooster was not beside her. The affection she felt for the communion of the Meek almost balanced his absence, except that she had missed the opportunity to ask him about his blind left eye. He seemed unaware of the loss. If he had acknowledged it, the deformation would not have diminished him a whit. He would still be hers. But ignorance separated them.

As much for the love of the sleeping Animals, then, as for comforting her own soul, Pertelote sang fully the ancient song that she had begun before:

> "Lullay lully, lully lulay,
> A fawcon hath borne my mate away.
>
> He bare hym up, he bare hym down,
> He bare him off on a thundercloud.
>
> And in that cloud there was a hall,
> Hangid all with a purpil pall.
>
> And in that hall there was a bed,
> Hangid with a veil so red.
>
> And in that bed there lythe a knyght,
> His wowndes bleeding day and nyght...."

[Thirteen]
In Which Wolves Appear

For Rachel, everything is good and nothing is bad.

Ferric Coyote has terrible suspicions regarding the stone chimney at the bottom of their rocky defile. It is as a "rocky defile" that he thinks of the tundra-hole in whose wall his pups were playing. To him the stones below led into a sewer pipe.

But Rachel? She says, "See what we have? Enough for all of us."

She was referring to the water droplets which was the steam's condensation on the facings above the ledge, water to quench five thirsty throats. And, moistened by the water, there sprouts a green shrub through a crevice in the rock. And, smiling on the slender branches of the shrub, there dark purple berries hung in the shapes of tiny apples. And all over the snouts of her three children are smears of purple juice.

What can Ferric do but streak south into the northern forests and watch for the dangers that love persuades him must lie in wait to endanger his family?

Forth and back. Forth and back—and, once before he dashes away, Rachel nuzzles him and says, "O Ferric, my unquiet defender. I pray that your son and your daughters live more tempered lives than yours."

But Rachel does not know what Ferric knows: that there *are* bad Creatures skulking throug the forest!

A White Wolf roams the frozen bracken.

Ferric hides and watches.

It could be that someone of more bulk and bravery might consider taunting the Wolf, maybe challenging the Wolf. But the Coyote's backbone is as thin as a zipper. His coat is rusty red, his cheeks retracted in a baleful grin, his black gums evident.

This Wolf foots the ground with stiff-legged threatfulness. He lifts his nose to the vagrant breezes. (Hide downwind, Ferric!) His white eyes flick the forest quicker than lightning. (See and not be seen, Coyote!)

For the love of his family, Ferric heaps courage upon courage and follows the White Wolf where he goes.

Forth and back. Then comes the night when the Wolf sits on his haunches in a small clearing, points his muzzle heavenward, narrows his slant eyes, rounds his lips, and howls.

Ferric's hot blood freezes.

The great White Wolf wails a long, long note. That note ascends by several harmonics until it finds a higher pitch.

The Coyote hides, his skinny butt bunched like a carving. Retreat is impossible. He grits his teeth.

Then the Wolf's ululation falls by a slow yodel into silence. Ferric too knows how to howl. He hears in this one an enticing invitation. Suddenly it breaks off. The Wolf stands up, his ears like cups turned to listening.

Another howl, a second howl, now echoes in the distance. Two howls. Two Wolves! Merciful heavens, must Ferric hide from a *pair* of Wolves? The Coyote's instincts battle inside his spirit. Run from the danger. Stay close to witness the danger.

The White Wolf raises his tail. He paws the ground in

anticipation. Then, out of the trees and into the clearing a *Black* Wolf arrives, her eyes shining like red fires in small lanterns. The Black Wolf walks to the White, grovels before him, and looks up into the face of the White Wolf, who lays the wrist of his forelegs across the other's neck, receiving her companionship. Both Wolves wag their tails. They nuzzle each other, making strange, squeaking sounds. Joy. This is a Wolvish joy. What does Ferric know of joy? The Black Wolf greets the White Wolf: "Boreas." The White Wolf answers, "Nota," and they begin to frisk like children.

Ferric searches his soul and finds two advantages. The predators do not know that he knows them. And he knows their names, but they don't know his. Knowing a name grant one some little power—if he has the fortitude to *call* that name aloud.

The night dissolves in dawn.

And all at once Ferric Coyote's thoughts are blown away. Not by his ears, but in his heart. He hears Rachel's voice, crying horror.

Rachel, crying for her son!

While his father is away Little Benoni has come to consider himself his mother's protector. Often the pup sneaks out of the den and out of the hole to stand on the tundra, watching.

Rachel is aware of her boy-cub's courage. He might *look* like Ferric, but now he's showing signs of a heart like Rachel's. Happy days!—they have a bold boy in their midst.

But on this particular morning when, half asleep, she assumes that Benoni has once again skittered topside, she does not know that he has, in fact, traipsed the big stones down to the bottom of the defile.

What brings her fully awake is a wordless twittering

outside the den. Some little somebody is frightened and crying as if within Rachel's ear, *Beware!*

Rachel frowns, then crawls out onto the ledge.

Why, it's a plain Brown Bird twitching up on stubby wings. The Bird darts at Rachel, then darts away.

"Good morning," Rachel says, hoping to calm the brown Bird down.

But the Bird will not be comforted.

Instead, she flies to Rachel's head and nips a whisker and tugs. She says aloud, "Zicküt!"

Come on, come on, and see what I see!

Then she releases the whisker and spirals in tight circles down into the rising steam, twittering anxiety.

Something's wrong.

Come down! See what I see!

Rachel follows the Brown Bird down.

"Zicküt!"

The Bird's voice makes a scratchy, unmusical sound, yet its meaning is clear.

In the moment when Rachel strikes bottom, she too is dismayed. The tip of Benoni's tail is just visible in the chimney pipe, and the pup is barkin, "Benoni has his eye on you!" Her son is as taut as his papa in freeze.

"Benoni!" Rachel cries. "Come out!"

But Benoni does not come out.

Rachel drives her snout into the black tunnel, her jaws open to snatch the pup's tail, but only succeeds in bumping him farther down.

Rachel raises howl in horror, "Benoni! Benoni!"

Suddenly pebbles fall, showering her. High above, where the pebbles have been dislodged, she hears, *"Tsssssst!"*

"Oh, Ferric!" she cries.

The little bird shoots up through the steam.

Ferric's voice barks, *"Yee-ouch!"*

Scramblings and thumpings announce his coming. Then he is beside her, the Brown Bird riding his skull and plucking hair with a bill as sharp as a needle.

"What, what?" Ferric dithers.

"Benoni's in the tunnel!"

Love overcomes fear. Without a thought Ferric plunges into the tunnel. "Benoni! Benoni!"

Then the tunnel is silent, as if it has swallowed both her husband and her son. Rachel holds her breath. The Brown Bird also floops into the tunnel.

Rachel gives voice to her anxiety. "Ferric!"

She hears the scratch of Coyote nails on stone.

First the Bird flies out. Then here comes Ferric dragging Benoni by the scruff of his neck, and Benoni with his eyes as wide as saucers.

Ferric zooms by Rachel and climbs the stony steps and does not stop until he drops his son on the ledge in front of the den.

At once the bony Coyote freezes. Rachel reaches them.

Benoni shakes himself. Saliva sprays his mother. The pup puts his nose to his father's nose. "Papa," he says, "I'm as brave as you."

[Fourteen]
In Which Outlanders
Gather at the Hemlock

A Jackrabbit appeared. He sat outside the Hemlock and waited, saying nothing. In her peregrinations Pertelote noticed the shock-eared Creature. She went to him and asked if he was hungry.

"Nope," said the Hare. "Yep," he said.

"I'll get some food for you."

"Nope, nope" he said. "Warrior Weasel told String Jack to talk to Him-What's-Lord-And-Captain-Of-All."

Pertelote said, "Chauntecleer isn't here right now."

The Hare's eyes were perpetually startled. His ears stood up like exclamation points—*Bang! Bang!*—declaring that ease was not a virtue.

"Said a Jack Rabbit should go to straight to the top. Said don't fuss with other Buggars."

Pertelote took an immediate liking to the fellow who seemed to believe that he had little to recommend himself, yet he dared the audience nonetheless. *Oh, see,* she smiled to herself, *how courageous a coward can be.*

At that moment Chauntecleer came circling down from the clouds and crowing Terce as he came.

String Jack jumped, He rocketed two hundred yards away, abruptly switched directions, and rocketed two hundred yards back again, where he stopped dead and peeped round-eyed up at the crowing Rooster.

"Him," said Pertelote, "what's Lord-and-Captain-of-All."

Finishing Terce, Chauntecleer cast his one eye down upon the visitor. He flew hither and landed, smiled and puffed out his chest.

"I suppose you've come for food," he said.

"Nope. Nope. Yep." String Jack, nerved, dropped a pile of poop-pellets.

Pertelote said, "John Wesley sent the Hare to us. He warned him to speak to none but you."

Chauntecleer nodded. It was always so.

"What, my friend," he said, "do you eat?"

"Sir. Sir. Twigs."

"Twigs, is it?"

The Rooster glanced around. "Pertelote, who has twigs?"

"We've got bark and berries and dried crustaceans. I don't know about twigs. His name is String Jack. Call him String Jack."

Chauntecleer thought a moment. Then he brightened and said, "Follow me, fellow. It's twigs you eat? It's twigs you'll have."

He went into the hall of the Hemlock and threw back his head and crowed. "Ratatosk Bore-Tooth! Come out of your house."

The shaggy nest five stories high shook as if someone had stamped his foot. "Go swallow sand, for all I care!"

"Come out," the Rooster crowed. "Rip twigs from your

walls and bring them here."

"Crack your gizzard on a *bag* of sand!"

"I'll crack your skull with my beak!"

"Chitter, chitter, chitter."

In a magisterial roar, Chauntecleer threatened the Squirrel. "I'll fly at you and tear your whole house down."

At the Rooster's thunder poor String Jack bolted and repeated his previous performance, leaping out of the hall, cornering and dodging, then hobbling back. A long-tailed Grey Squirrel was descending the trunk of the Hemlock, bunches of rough twigs stuffed in his jowls.

"And what," he spat, "is Ratotosk to eat in return?"

"Poop-pellets."

When the Hen Pertelote returned to her business, walking out of the Hemlock hall, Chauntecleer trimmed his steps to hers.

"I expect we'll crowd this place before long."

"I expect you're right, Chauntecleer."

"And none will go hungry."

Pertelote paused. So did the Rooster. His eye gazed proudly into the future. Her eyes regarded him.

"Oh," Chauntecleer said, "what good days these are."

For the moment she kept her thoughts to herself.

"And Wyrm," he announced, "will finally be destroyed."

This surprised her.

"Haven't we finished with the monster?"

"Oh, my beloved, no. Feeding the world is just a beginning. *Cleansing* the world shall be my more glorious feat."

"Husband?" she asked softly, for she sensed mortal pride in his mood. "No one can cleanse the world of wickedness."

Chauntecleer beamed graciously down upon her. "Beautiful Pertelote, place your faith in me. I have been granted an orphic knowledge. Mine it is to grant the whole world peace."

"Lord Chauntecleer," Pertelote said, "you look at me with your right eye only. Show me your left."

"I can't. It's blind."

She was taken aback. "Then you know."

"Of course I know. Haven't I always been the master of my own body?"

But Pertelote seemed to have the better memory. No. There were times when Chauntecleer had not been master of his body, let alone of his emotions.

"Chauntecleer," she said, "How did your left eye lose its sight?"

He laughed a grand laugh. "It's a long, long story, Pertelote, too long to tell it now. But here's the gist of the thing. Recently I discovered wisdom in Wyrmesmere. I asked the sea to give me a portion of its treasure. The sea asked for something in return—and for the sake of the Creatures of the world I honored the request. 'Throw the sight of one eye into my waters 'and I will make you wise.' And lo, blindness bought me a path that stretches from my feet all the way to glory."

Pertelote tried to understand, but failed. His explanation had the effect of estranging him the more from her.

"Chauntecleer, do you love me?"

He boomed with laughter. "Would I devote my life to the thing that very well could *take* my life, if I didn't love you?"

"My Lord, I have loved the you that has always been you. No amount of grandeur can increase my love."

"Faith, faith, dear Pertelote!" the Rooster proclaimed. "Now then," he said, "I have to go."

She wanted to ask, "But when will you be back?"—except that he had so swiftly departed.

•   •   •

Animals came. Animals referenced a boisterous Weasel, and came.

Pertelote, the mistress of the community and the receiver of the hungry, lost herself in her duties.

The outside boughs of the Hemlock were sheathed in ice. It soared heavenward like a polished tower. When the wind blew hard, ice crystals struck the ground like tiny xylophones, and though the tree might sway, it neither cracked nor broke, and the frozen interior contained a most comofrting warmth.

There came to the woods near the Hemlock a Creature, a distant cousin of John Wesley Weasel. He was a Marten sleek and long, whose name was Selkirk. He kept himself to himself. It was only the beautiful Pertelote who knew of his presence. This was an Animal who roamed the marchlands alone. He dwelt at the outermost boundaries of every society, in uninhabitable wastelands. It must have been a violent hunger that drew him toward the oppression of too many Beasts all in one place.

What would he eat?

He didn't answer because to speak words out loud seemed to unsap him. He shot up a spruce and lay on a top limb.

Pertelote moved in and out of the great hall, arranging smaller and smaller meals for the hungry since Chauntecleer's larders would have to last the long winter through. Pertelote comforted the famished and offered solace to the broken. Yet a piece of the Hen continued to suffer the veil between her husband and herself. What she did, she did very well. But a sensitive soul could perceived the yearning underneath.

When the night arrived without a sign of Chauntecleer, Pertelote flew with two swipes of her wings to the limb she shared with her husband when he was home, tried to compose herself. Think, think: what should she sing to accomplish this night's ending?

Oh, Chauntecleer!

"Lady Hen?"

Not Chauntecleer. It was a Mouse.

"You up there, Lady Hen?"

Pertelote answered, "I am here."

"Want some buddies?"

Seven buddies, to be exact. Then, to put a good face on her restlessness, she said, "I never knew that Mouses flew."

"Hee hee," said one Mouse. "Hee hee," the others joined in. "A pretty good joke for a sad Lady Hen."

Sad? What did they know?

"My dear cadets," she said, "why do you think I need friends right now?"

"Well"—this was Freitag—"me and my brothers, we don't want to be botherations. But we see that the Lady Hen is not happy."

"It's the night," she said. "Even our visitors are asleep. You should be asleep as well. I promise you, I can manage."

So, seven Mice said, "Good night. Good night. Sweet dreams," and, "Don't let the bedbugs bite."

She heard little skitterings below. And soon her little comforters were sleeping too.

Pertelote admired them. She sent her voice like a silver flute abroad.

> "The summer's courtship's long gone by,
> Those evenings when my Lord and I
>   Were young.
> He took my tears on faith and I
> Would stroke his neck, and I would sigh
>   This song:

'Come peel a straw, a summer's thistle,
Blow on it and make it whistle
   Dreams.'
And I? I never said he couldn't
Build a world secure with wooden
   Beams."

[Fifteen]
John's Pure Joy

Oh, the Weasel was in his element now!

There was nowhere where the winter was not, nor anywhere where Critters did not worry about their next meals. Vast territories awaited John's good news. And who didn't love a Good-News-Bringer?

"Hoopla, furry buggars! Gots vittles? Well, Him-What's-Lord-and-Captain of All—he *gots* the vittles!"

Often it was his personal vigor that persuaded the hungry to leave their homes and travel to the Hemlock, where ("Bet on it, Buggars") they would find a hearty welcome.

"An acorn? Bite it. Sarsaparilla? Nip it. Sagebrushes? Stuff you mush-mouths full of it."

Oh, so many Critters, shivering in their nesty denny houses, in the hollows of trees, in burrows under stone. Some, slack-eyed, had surrendered themselves to dying. John's pity empowered him.

Those that could go, he asked to help them that could not go.

In a grove of aspen trees he came upon a Stag lying beside his daughter. John made friends by asking their names, always saying his name first: "John Double-u of the Double-u's, fearsome warrior is he." Then, fearlessly asking "What's a Double-u to call a Stag by?"

The Stag answered that his name was Black-Pale-on-a-Silver Field. The child panting against her father's chest he named The Fawn De La Coeur.

Under other circumstances, Black-Pale would have cut a noble figure. His head was dignified with two eight-pointed antlers, his shoulders glossy and strong, his haunches able to drive him forward by long, sailing leaps.

But his eyes were stricken.

In the day when the earth had trembled the Fawn's mother fell, breaking her right foreleg. Soon Fimbul-winter had defeated the Doe, who on the third day perished. Now De La Coeur was herself feverish, panting faster than a Rabbit. Her father had gathered the baby to himself as though he would be her last abode.

As soon as he heard their grim tale, John Wesley began to rush around the pair, nattering, barking, thrusting a paw into the air, crying, "Do and do and do!"

Black-Pale remained aground. He murmured that his prayers were for his daughter, that she should meet a swift and painless death.

What did John know of subtleties? Compassion in the Weasel looked like anger. He buffeted the Stag's snout. He pranced down the Stag's neck, his back and his butt.

"Papa, he loves his baby? Papa's what loves is papa's what saves pretty little Critters!" He smacked the Stag on his chin.

Black-Pale lifted his head, lifted the grand branches of his antlers, and bugled, "Let go. Run away! Leave us to die in peace."

Rather than frightened, the Weasel was delighted. "See? Papa, he gots him fire! Do and do, Papa! Up and fight him what's a fearsome warrior!"

Black-Pale heaved himself to standing on all four hooves. Razor-sharp, those hooves could cut a Weasel in half. But John laughed. "Hoopla!" he cried and danced away. "Fight! Fight, poor bumfuzzled Papa! Fightings and foinings and hoopla! Is a Stag what's life-ly again!"

All at once the Weasel began to sing. No subtlety this. A garbage can could make such a noise. John's mind might have been civilized—but his voice was barbarian.

> *"Gots eatables and sweetables*
> *For babies sad with troubables—"*

Then it was not Black-Pale, stamping the ground, intent on bruising a Weasel. It was the Weasel himself who noticed that the Fawn had opened her eyes.

So he threw himself into a louder yell:

> *"Gots what's good at roostering,*
> *And Hens what roots and toots and things—"*

John Wesley careered through the aspens, dodging the flashing black hooves. The Stag snorted in frustration—but then both battlers stopped and tipped their ears to listen. It sounded as if little bubbles were bursting back of the aspens.

And then it was a bell-like music.

The Fawn De La Coeur, she was giggling at the silly scene the adults were making.

Black-Pale ambled over to her. He lowered his magnificent head and nuzzled her neck with his moist nose.

"Oh, Papa," De La Coeur said, twinkling, "you are so handsome."

So, then: on and on John Wesley traveled through the territories, sporting for pure joy, going and coming with goodnesses and with fine solutions for Critters everywhere.

[Sixteen]
In Which an Ancient Prophecy is Retold

Once again Chauntecleer was keeping his midnight appointments, each one of which increased the heat in his veins, for the time was at hand.

Above the wide, tarry island that rode the face of the sea, there glowed a gaseous rouge-red light, the *ignis fatuus* of wisdom.

Quem mittam? sang the sea in the language of the Powers. Whom shall I send?

The sea was teaching Chauntecleer how to answer: *Ecce ego, mitte me.*

"Here I am. Send me."

Soon, my son, the sea sang fatherly. "Soon the sign shall be shown to you. Galle superbe, you will hear it in the mouth of the humblest of Creatures. He shall point you to the portal of the cathedrals of Wyrm, and courage shall not shrink from the deed before you.

• • •

The gross, lifeless corpse of Monstrous Hatred was decaying. It was the gasses of his corruption and the oils thereof that were boiling up through fissures in the mantel of the earth, through nozzles in the sea's bed. The corrupt gasses seethed, and gouts of bitumen lay on the waters.

Et ambulabo in latitudine.

And I will walk in liberty.

The kiss may have killed the Serpent. But his cunning mind lived on, causing the ocean to talk.

There is an ancient prophecy:

Should ever the Animals fail and their species perish, God would repeople the earth by weeping. His tears would fall from heaven and pot the dry clay, raising dust-puffs where they hit. Every one of God's tears would moisten its spot of clay, turning dirt into a red daub, and every daub into a new race of two-legged beings.

Which is to say, God would try again.

[Seventeen]
In Which the Weasel Reaches the Boreal Forests

By now John Wesley Weasel thinks he is nearing the end of his assignment, because the populations have thinned and he has traveled miles without meeting another hungry tummy.

A one-eared Creature can sometimes miscalculate the direction from which a sound is coming. A body needs two ears to find its distant source. To John Wesley most noises seem to come from one side of him. Therefore he has to adjust by spinning in circles.

Now, as he is spinning in circles in the gloaming of the forest, several Creatures have set up a howling—remote and barely audible. Could be six or seven Creatures, by their awful harmonies. Wolves. It causes him sadness, for they are singing elegies.

Heartbreak lends speed to his legs. John dashes around pine trees, over ridges, and through jumbles of fallen logs. He tracks the spoor of one Wolf. The howling reduces to yaps and mewings, then, suddenly, all the voices fall silent. The silence feels premonitory.

Then John surprises himself by bounding out of the forest and into a clearing. He pulls up in front three Wolves. They sensed the Weasel's approach and meet him now stiff-legged and war, rigid, their heads lowered, their snouts wrinkled, their upper lips curled back showing their fangs.

But John Double-u (that mighty warrior) is equal to any situation.

"Wolfies saved!" he announces. "John, he brings good news. Is food, Wolfies!"

Whoa! Three Wolves can sound like a whole chorus?

There is a White Wolf whose eyes are white, their pupils round, black pits. And Black Wolf with red eyes, and a Brown Wolf, yellow-eyed.

The White Wolf gathers his feet and lunges.

The Weasel hip-hops sideways, so the Wolf comes down on the tip of the Weasel's tail, which loses a hank of fur.

"Hey! Double-u's is not for biting! Isn't eatables. Not 'gestables neither. But John, he can say where eatables *is.* "

The Weasel has flash-quick eyes. When the White Wolf made his lunge, John saw a fourth Wolf lying loose and dead behind the other two.

"Oh," he whispers. "Oh, Wolfies. John, he knows—" knows why they were howling elegies.

Perhaps it is his genuine compassion that shootes the White Wolf's aggression.

John moves mournfully toward the dead Creature. He pats her great head and sniffs a dribble back into nose.

"What," he says, "is dead Wolfie's name?"

The Black Wolf answers, "Favonius."

It is Lord Chauntecleer who knows the Crows for funerals and the prayers that lighten every darkness. John has never had the gall to sing them himself. But situations force impossibilities.

Whether or not he has the right, whether or not God would accept a Double-u's prayer, he does what he cannot do. John Wesley sings.

> "Lordy God, we begs you
> To bright-light Wolfies' sadnesses;
> And all nights, all nights long
> Please wipe our poor hurtings away."

Ferric Coyote, hiding beneath a Lodge-Pole Pine, weeps when he hears the Weasel's threnody. Tensions may deny all moods but fear. But this particular kindness moves him.

Such a brave Creature! He sings to Wolves as if they were family. He teaches them where to find food, and they listen, and they go, and the forest is empty of threat.

Ferric feels sympathy tickling in one nostril, and he sneezes.

John says, "What? Is a Who somewhere in there?"

Ferric freezes hard as rock. He has revealed his hiding place, has given up his advantage.

Soon he hears a tick-nailed scramble, and the Weasel appears.

"Well, lookeehere! Is a woody Coyote and a buttable rump high's a tent."

The Weasel crouches and touches Ferric's nose with his own. He whispers, "Does woody Coyotes sleeps with his eyeballs open?"

The Weasel puffs at Ferric's eyes, and Ferric blinks.

"Hoopla! Is awake! John, he knows wakefulnesses." He crouches before Ferric's snout."Woody Coyote might-be wants food?"

Ferric heard the Weasel's promises to the Wolves. And the

dangerous Animals believed him. Ferric saw malice drain from their muscles, replaced by need alone.

Suddenly hiding seems a silly proposition.

Then John Wesley is indeed at the end of his assignment, for he has come to the bleak, windswept and empty tundra. It is here that he finally permits his weariness to overcome him. He hopes to spend some time sleeping in the Coyotes' den.

But a gaggle of little Coyotes rouse him from slumber. Three Coyote-lings. The boy-Coyote wants to play-fight, and displays bravery by his tiny attacks. John Double-u laughs and cuffs the kid and nips him right back.

Their mother smiles blessings upon their happy scrambling. A pleasant woman, this host who straightway finds in the Weasel a friend.

Papa Woody-Coyote, he sits on the hard snow above. He gets up and paces, darts there, darts here, sits grimly again, made most unhappy by the noise of cheerfulness and by the dangerous clatter of carelessnesses.

The boy-pup flies at John, yelling, "Benoni to the rescue!" Kid's name is Benoni.

"To rescuings?" says John. "Is for rescuings from *what?*"

Benoni goes to the ledge in front of the den. He tells the Weasel to look down. At the bottom is a wide throat releasing steam. He tells John about the big stone steps and about the tunnel that goes deep, deep underground.

"Badness lives down there," whispers Benoni Coyote. "When I went into that tunnel, Mrs. Bird-friend scared me and mama scolded me."

[Eighteen]
In Which the Weasel of Good News Returns with More Good News

In one sense the Hemlock had become an infirmary. The Animals last to arrive had come sick with starvation, their ribs visible under the fur. Pertelote laid them close between the wooly Sheep, and she nursed them with her medicinals.

A noble Stag arrived bearing his daughter on his back. The Fawn's eyes had crusted shut. She asked Chalcedony to peck gently the yellow crust until her sight had been restored.

Slow Moles came.

Wolves came, but kept their distance.

The home-Creatures served all of these while Pertelote carried food to that world-rim-walker, the Marten Selkirk.

In another sense, then, the Hemlock hall was a frugal refectory, for the Mr. and Mrs. Cobbs and the Hens doled out small portions of food. The ice the Animals brought inside melted and satisfied a thousand thirsts.

What the hall had *not* become was a charnel house.

Absolutely no one died—which salved the wound in Pertelote's soul, for Chauntecleer may have been Crowing the Canonical Crows, but he often left the burgeoning community to its own devices and the daily business to herself.

And then another salve bounded into the hall: John Wesley Weasel, bringing with him the joy of a job accomplished.

"Hilla hilla *ho*, Lady Hen!"

"Oh, John. Oh, John, you're back."

"Back with gleefulnesses, on account of, lookee: all John's *friends* is here."

Tick-Tock boomed, "Huzzah for a friends!"

And all his armies shouted, "Huzzah!"

The Brothers Mice tumbled and pummeled the Weasel's noggin.

"Hey! Mices! John's head, it's not no punch bag!"

Skinny Chalcedony smiled.

Jasper glowered. "Ain't no one asked Jasper did she want to give up her three squares a day. Ain't no one gave Jasper a thought."

John Wesley whooped, "Gots to see the Rooster! Lady Hen, where's a Rooster for John to be seeing?"

Pertelote suffered the moment, then she answered, "I don't know."

"Doesn't know where he goes?"

"South, John. He flies south That's all I can tell you."

"Hoopla!" cried John, and shot from the Hemlock off to the south.

South and yet farther south, until the Weasel found himself on the ravaged land where the Coop once stood. He rejoiced in the place, and mourned it too, for here had been his martial successes. But here the Wee Widow Mouse had perished.

South and south, and then John Wesley heard the *Whump* of a sea wave. It seemed to say, *Quem mittam?*

Of course the Weasel knew nothing of the language of the Powers. But he knew his Rooster's crow when he heard it, and he heard it now: *"Mitte me!"*

Off again, racing across the earth-scar.

And there was the Rooster, soaring golden above the ocean and under the bellies of the clouds, causing them to glow.

John grinned at the sight. Lord Chauntecleer was riding thermals like an Eagle.

Chauntecleer heard the waters below say, "Heed me! Your sign, my son, is on the beach."

Immediately the Rooster trimmed his flight. He swooped into a wide spiral, scanning the white, salty beach of Wyrmesmere. He saw John Wesley Weasel jumping up and down, throwing his paws up in delight.

"My gallant chevalier!" Chauntecleer laughed, alighting beside the Weasel. "My messenger gone, and my messenger home again, home from the perils of exploration!"

Against every tendency in poor John's character, he sobbed. Oh, the joy of his great Lord's praise.

"Ah," said Chauntecleer, touching a tear. "Even so much do you love me."

John nodded. He quickly figured that it was no weakness, here and out of the sight of the Animals, to reveal his affections in such a girlish manner.

"Weep your weepings," the Rooster said. "I am nothing if not patient. Purpose has given me patience. But as soon as you can, tell me the message you bring."

John Wesley grinned. He swallowed the raw lump in his

throat, dredged up his voice, and croaked: "Is a family Coyote what John's gots to feed. He gots to go back."

Chauntecleer paused, frowning.

"This isn't what I want to hear."

"Is a den farthestmost north, and nothings north of that," John said. "Woody Coyote, he says, No, no. He won't come. So John, he gots to go there."

Chauntecleer's frown became baleful. "This," he said, "is no sign, John Wesley. This is not what I want to hear."

The Weasel jabbered faster and faster: "Woody Coyote, he won't come, on account of, it's a hole where the den is, and it's a deep, deep tunnel under that, and little kid Benoni Coyote showed John the tunnel. Little kid Coyote, he tells John what is down there. Says, Wickedness is down there. Wickedness inside the earth."

Chauntecleer's neck snapped straight. He glanced toward the sea. "John!" he crowed a glorious crow. *"That's* what I want to hear!"

Lord Chauntecleer settled on the highest spire of the Hemlock tree.

"All is well!" he crowed. "And all will be better than well. All my company,I pledge you my oath. All the world shall be cleansed of Hatred, of Evil. I go to execute the heinous Wyrm!"

All the Animals crowded out of the Hemlock hall and filled the fields beyond.

Chauntecleer was sunlight.

Pertelote looked, and grieved.

"None need worry," the Rooster declared. "None need follow me. I go to win your salvation. I will select two only to go with me, but neither one to fight with me. They shall be my passage north. John Wesley Weasel, lead me to the tunnel.

Black-Pale-On-A-Silver-Field, bear me thither that I might save my strength for the conquest."

Unto glory went the Rooster, riding the Stag whose nobility was meant to herald the puissance of this Crusader's weapons: Gaff, his sharp and shining left spur, and the Slasher, his right.

Pertelote watched the departure. Her husband rode Black-Pale's antlers as if he rode a chariot.

"Wyrm!" She heard his voice as they cantered over the horizon. "Forsake your soul!"

For the rest of that day Pertelote wandered away from the Hemlock.

If her grief was evident, if was casting a pall over the company she had deserted, she didn't know.

At night she sailed silently her roost.

No one crowed the Canonical crows.

At midnight she was moved to sing, though quietly, under her breath:

> "—made love to me so slow and sweetly,
> Singing names, he came discreetly
>   Home.
> And I to him gave children after;
> I it was had cried through laughter,
>   Come—"

PART FOUR

Chauntecleer:
When Weal Is Woe

[Nineteen]
'I'm Going to Lose Him,' She Thinks, 'Too Soon. Too Soon.'

Benoni Coyote has stopped his life of play and has grown more serious than is natural for one so young.

His father's refusal to go with the Weasel (as Benoni himself would gladly have gone) gave the little Coyote pause. The Weasel was a Creature filled with hilarities and good will. Coyotes should trust such a someone—as Ferric seemed to do when he first came. But when the Weasel suggested that Ferric leave the den, Benoni's papa's spine went rigid. He crouched in alarm. And now that John Weasel has taken off for the south, Benoni sees an odd collision of feelings in his father. A guilty Coyote, maybe? For not having braved the journey? A troubled Coyote? For not finding food? A desperate Coyote. Benoni's papa seems to want to protect his family more fiercely than ever before—on account of what?

Twill and Hopsacking are losing weight. They drink the steam's water, but the bush has withered, and they have nothing left to eat. Even his mother doesn't smile. She stays with her daughters inside the den. She tells them tales to distract them. Sometimes one of his sisters will nip at her mother's cheek, begging for food, and Rachel will try to regurgitate some little something and fail. There was nothing left in his mama's tummy.

With a mother's love she conceals her worries. She ends each tale with a prayer. "Rest, my children. God will bless you, and I'll be here in the morning."

Actually, Rachel is doing more than comforting her daughters. She is watching her son too, and feels his burden. What was the boy-cub thinking these days?

"I'm going to lose him," she thinks, "too soon."

For he doesn't tease his sisters anymore. When the plain Brown Bird (whom the children call Auntie) comes to visit, Benoni doesn't greet her. He seems oblivious of her presence.

Rachel asks, "Do you think your Auntie is too silly for you?"

"No'm."

"Do your sisters annoy you?"

"No'm."

"What's happening, Noni?"

"Nothing."

Rachel gazes at his soft, earnest face. "I don't think that it is nothing. I think you want to grow up before your time."

Benoni looks away from his mother's gaze. "I," he mumbles. "I have jobs to do."

Comes the morning when Rachel hears the sound of a little Coyote gone. She springs from the den.

"Noni? Benoni?"

Her immediate fear is that he's run down the decline again, braving the tunnel and the denizen below.

"Benoni! You'll kill yourself down there!"

The plain Brown Bird flies down and says, "Zicküt!"

She flutters in front of Rachel. "Zicküt! Zicküt!"

The boy is not by the portal again.

"Please," Rachel cries, "watch my daughters."

The icy tundra is grand and deadly. Rachel dashes into the dark interior of the forest.

"Benoni!"

Echoes laugh. Ice cracks. A load of crystal crashes to the ground, and Rachel runs headlong.

"Benoni!"

As she goes she noses the ground, trying to find her baby's spoor.

"Benoni, tell me where you are!"

She hears a faint wail to her left. She stops and holds still. Again the wail. It sounds so vulnerable. Rachel breaks in that direction. She takes extraordinary leaps over hillocks and across ditches. Quick, efficient arcs around the pine.

"Mama!"

Benoni! It's you!"

Then here comes her son like a red pellet with serious eyes. They thumps into his mother's bosom and pushes and pushes as if to crawl inside.

"Benoni, what *is* this? Why did you run away?"

The young Coyote mews in her fur.

She steps back. "Were you lost?"

He nods and bursts into tears: "Hoo, hooooo."

Oh, how tightly Rachel gathers her son to herself, under her chin, against her breast.

"Oh, Benoni, I was so afraid for you."

Ice slides from the treetops and smashes the ground like bones and glass. Benoni shivers.

"Why did you run away? Didn't you know that this is a lonely world?"

The child beneath her neck says, "Yes'm. I knew." Gravely he explains, "It's why I came."

She sees her son in her mind: his face-fur standing out like a soft sunburst, his tail no more than a trigger cocked. But he is a deep Coyote.

"What? To be hurt?"

"No'm. To help papa."

"Whisht. So you think your papa needs help?"

She feels his small head nod.

"You think papa is weak?"

"No. Not weak. He is…. Mama, he is afraid. I came to help him fight enemies. But I got lost."

"Benoni, Benoni."

Soon, she thought behind the wash in her eyes. *Too soon.*

[Twenty]
A Legend

There stands at the edge of time the Eschaton-Bull. His head hangs low from a muscled hump. His nostrils blow a red smoke. The horns that curve from his shaggy hair seem to be too small for one so big and so mighty.

It is the Bull's slow molting that numbers the years. For every one hair shed, one year passes by. One hundred haiars are a century, one thousand a millennium.

When one of his legs break, that marks an eon gone.

At the end of three ages, the Eschaton-Bull must balance on a single leg. This is his last leg.

And that is the saying the Animal's know.

[Twenty-One]
Chauntecleer's Descent

The StagBlack-Pale stands at the edge of a rocky defile. The crown in the forest of his antlers is the golden Chauntecleer. Chauntecleer gazes down at the family before him and greets the male with a grave formality.

"Ferric, I presume?"

Straightway the rusty Coyote suffers lockjaw.

Chauntecleer thinks, *What ails this red poltroon?*

John Wesley dashes happily to the female.

"Salue-bretations, Mama! Is a tried-and-blue-true Double-u what's come back again!"

John jumps about and spreads food on the ground: a bundle of honey-soaked reeds. "Sweet, sweet, *sweet!*" For the kids he opens a bag of ice cream.

"Isn't only-est a Fox what knows tricks," John exults. Oh, he is so glad to be with the kids again. "Is a John Double-u, too!" He puts on the face of a serious instructor and instructs. "Is in springtime, cubby-kids. Bark of a cottonwood—rip it off! White of the woodiness inside—scrape and scrape the pretty white sap-foam! Pretty white sap-foam—bag it! Is in wintertime—freeze it! Hoopla! Ice cream!"

Black-Pale keeps his own counsel. His motive for allowing the Rooster to ride the tines of his antlers has had little to do with the Rooster wishes because that one has been imperious, scarcely acknowledging the Stag's nobility. No, it was for the sake of the Weasel that he has come. For John Wesley, who brought cheer to the Fawn De La Coeur and who persuaded Black-Pale to carry his daughter south to a healing ward where she was brought back to health again. And isn't it the better part of nobility to serve good heart without expecting a return?

The boy-cub—Benoni?—neglects the ice cream and trots to Black-Pale. He says to the golden Cock, "Papa's tired." Then the little Coyote bows his little head, and the Stag recognizes honor in the gesture.

Chauntecleer says, "I have been informed, boy, that you have found, and yourself have half-entered, the tunnels that open the way to the Wickedness that dwells in the earth. Is this true?"

Benoni nods.

"A hero, then, of the first waters."

Two reactions: the boy-cub grows sober and pulls himself up to full height. The female Coyote whispers, "Don't believe it, Benoni."

John Wesley seconds Chauntecleer. "John," he tips, "he's seen a kid's dauntlessnesses, yes! Yes! And John, he *knows*. Tough little Benoni! Brave little Benoni!"

Chauntecleer's voice grows suddenly strident. "Enough of banter. I've come to enter the netherworld. Benoni, Coyote! Show me your tunnels."

"Yessir."

Rachel cries, "*No* sir!"

"Silence, woman! Benoni, go."

At the Rooster's command Benoni drops over the

cleft onto the den-ledge and prepares to scramble the steps into steam.

Rachel leaps after him and shrieks, "No! I will not lose you!"

From nowhere a Brown Bird appears and flies into the boy-cub's face.

"Auntie!" Benoni tries to slap her away "Let me go!"

"Zickǔt!" With her long bill the Bird yanks hairs out of his ears.

"Ouchy! *Ouchy!*"

Chauntecleer touches Black-Pale's neck with the points of his spurs. "Go!"

John Wesley shouts to everyone, "Is okay! Woody-Coyotes, the Rooster, he *gots* to go down. Is to murder Wyrm, and nobodies, nobodies ever hurts again."

Rachel pleads, "Let *me* show the way."

"Zickǔt!" the Brown Bird insists through her scorched voice. "Zichǔt! Zichǔt!"

Rachel, I will go. You watch out for the children.

Least flies urgently back and forth between Chauntecleer and the rocky defile. It's not long before the Rooster understands that she has become his guide.

The Rooster drives both spurs into Black-Pale's neck. The Stag wants to rear up and shake the Cock from his antlers, except that John Wesley is tumbling after the Bird and crying everyone forward. And the Cock has, in fact, almighty strength and an ineluctable purpose.

So three Creatures plunge into the vomiting cloud. Black-Pale is as sure-footed as a Bighorn Ram. He never falters on the stones. Chauntecleer strikes the rocky sides of the defile with Gaff and the Slasher, who spark and ring and are sharpened.

"Behold, Wyrm! Behold, I come!"

Athousand hissings answer: *"Veni, mortalis. Et pere."*

Come, thou mortal. And die.

Then the Brown Bird comes to a fluttering hover. The tunnel is immediately beneath her. And the air therein, having not yet met the cold, is clear.

John Wesley cries, "Do and do and do!"

Chauntecleer responds with cold command, "This is mine."

He wings down from Black-Pale's antlers and passes through the portal alone.

Chauntecleer slits his eye, but sees nothing. The floor and the walls are path enough. They seem to have been carved in marble.

Saluto te, a myriad spigots hiss in the depths of the earth. Welcome.

Chauntecleer's flight is not foreshortened. His energies do not abate. If it took ten days he would not rest.

Soon he spies a vague light ahead. An amber glowing. His heart beats wildly. His mind enters that zone of absolute focus, where the world slows down like a ponderous metronome, and he himself is speed, the thing itself.

The tunnel widens. Chauntecleer finds himself in a cathedral-like cavern, The amber light is now as round as a rose window. And lying like great cable upon the floor of the nave, Wyrm!

Chauntecleer murmurs, "I am for you now."

The Lord Rooster spreads his mighty wings. He soars from the amber light into the pitchy heights, directly over the skull of his Foe.

Like the Hawk, Chauntecleer tilts and swoops down. Just before he hits flesh, the glorious Rooster catches air beneath his wings, doubles his hocks and, holds the points of his weapons foremost

"Damn you!" he cries spears the skull of Wickedness.

But there comes no cry of outrage.

And the spurs don't cut tough, living tissue. Instead, they sink into a pulpy rot. Chauntecleer's momentum takes him likewise into the mire of Wyrm's dead flesh. Valiant Chauntecleer is enveloped by an oily putrefaction. When he struggles to find a way out, he falls instead into a chamber of amber light.

Chauntecleer guts spasm. Over and over again he vomits a bilious, fetid gore. Where his vomit splashes the ground, it puts out a host of the tiny amber lights. But other lights, a myriad of lights, cover the walls and the ceiling of the chamber.

Chauntecleer peers at them and realizes what they are. Maggots! Thin tendrils attached to every surface. All together, they mark the shape of the room in which the Rooster stands, and he realizes the truth.

The is Wyrm's eye socket. Massy Wyrm is already dead.

Chauntecleer has been denied his glory.

A voice says, *Sing.*

Voices say, *What shall we sing?*

The voice says, *Of the hero who dared the depths of the earth.*

Multitudinous tendril worms say, *Eum laudamus.*

We do. We praise him.

The voice says, *O Galle magne, tu es filius meus dilectus.*

O great Rooster, thou art my most darling son.

And again that singular voice says, *Si me filius mei liberavit, vere liber ero.*

If my son sets me free, I will be free indeed.

[Twenty-Two]
In Which the Weasel Follows

Both John Wesley and Black-Pale-On-A-Silver-Field have obeyed Chauntecleer's command to remain among the stones before portal that opens into the tunnel that leads into the underworld. They've waited a day and a night and now the half of a second day. And though the Weasel would have loved to share confidences with the Stag, Black-Pale has been keeping his own counsel and has not answered. Finally John shut up too and slumped into an anxiety on behalf of his Rooster.

Indeed, it is a tremendous undertaking, to slay ancient Hatred. And it surely must take time to complete. But this was too *much* time.

John believes in Chauntecleer. Didn't the Rooster schooled him in social behaviors? And wasn't it the Rooster who praised a Weasel's guts and fighting? Do and do and do for you, slithery little Buggars. By which John meant the Basilisks. It was glorious Chauntecleer who led them in the war to victory.

But what if the Rooster were overcome? What if he lay dead...?

• • •

Not at speed, not dashing, but restraining himself, John Russel creeps down the long marble tunnel. If Chauntecleer is still engaged in his war for the world, John will not intrude. *Zoom*, he will shoot straight back and up.

Down the marble hallway, and counting the time as he goes. If it's taking John Wesley this long, well, maybe that's the reason for the Rooster's malingering.

The Weasel listens for sounds below. But he hears nothing of battle. He hears no cries of victory.

Soon the tunnel begins to widen. John sees something ahead of him, but it is so vague it could be a dream.

John has always been fearless. But this subterranean cave makes a sound that is no sound at all. It is like the air in a vast cathedral which oppresses the ears. That amber light is ghastly. The air smells like candle-smoke when the monks have pinched their wicks and left the room in a monastic silence. Not fearful, then, but wary. Oh, how he admires his Lord Chauntecleer's audacity!

John creeps across a rock-hewn floor toward a cavern where glows the soft amber light.

There! There! There sits the Rooster! Like a saint in a shell of sacred glory!

But he isn't moving. And his feathers are no longer golden. They are slimy with the oils of corruption.

John Wesley begins to run to his Lord Chauntecleer. Just before he reaches the amber chamber, he kicks something that goes rattling away. A bone. John Wesley feels across the floor and finds more bones. He squints and makes out a skull. By the tissue where its nose once was the Weasel sees how gigantic that nose must have been.

He yells, "Mundo Cani!"

Now the Rooster moves.

"Who's out there?"

"Me, Chanti-cleer! John Double-u."

"You disobeyed me!"

"Is a John what comes, might-be, to help a Rooster."

"You said Mundo Cani!"

The Rooster's angry. Why should the Rooster be angry?

"Is fightings all done? Did the Rooster, he kill Wyrm?"

"Wyrm is dead."

With little conviction the Weasel says, "Hoopla." And with false bravado says, "Cut for cut. The Rooster, he won the day."

Why then should Chauntecleer be angry if he did what he came to do?

"Weasel! You said Mundo Cani's name! Why?"

"On account of...."

But this is such a sad thing to say, for John remembers that it was the Rooster's purpose also to bring the Hound home again, alive.

"Dammit, Weasel, *why?*"

"Is bones."

"What? What did you say?"

John Wesley raises his sorrowful voice and yells, "Is the Dog's bones down here."

For the space of a minute Chauntecleer stands inside the glowing chamber with his beak open, stunned.

Then he roars, "Get the hell out of here! Leave me alone!"

John Wesley does not obey. He is bewildered. Uncertainly he says, "Rooster, he comes too."

"I deny you, Weasel! I refuse to let pettiness look upon the disaster I have become! Run! Run before I tear pettiness to pieces!"

Again, John Wesley cannot obey. No matter disasters. No matter defeats. How can the Animals survive without a leader to lead them?

Old boldness takes hold of the Weasel's heart again.

"So *tear* a Weasel to pieces!" he yells. "Try a Weasel! Is a Weasel what will fight you!" And he adds, "Bastard!"

Chauntecleer turns his head away from John Wesley. He withdraws inside himself. He sits, his wings slick oil. Miserably he says, "Oh, leave me alone."

John is dancing on two paws, striking the air with his fists. "Fight and fight and fight a Weasel!"

But it does not rouse Chauntecleer.

"John, he says spit on a Rooster! He says *piss* on a Rooster! But John, he gots to stay here till a Rooster, he *don't* stay here no more."

Can it be? Is Chauntecleer weeping tears? Oh, no, no! Look at those tears. They are sliding tendrils of amber worms falling from his eyes.

John Wesley will not be done until it is good and done. He picks up a thigh-bone of the Dog and hurls it at Chauntecleer. It skids across a paste of worms. He throws pay-bones like dice. They rain on the Rooster, who does not move. Finally the Weasel heaves up Mundo Cani skull and runs with it into Chauntecleer's chamber and drops it on the Rooster's head.

Chauntecleer stands and looks at the thing. Then, slowly, he wraps his wings around it, sits, and begins to rock.

"I can't," he whimpers. "I can't even confess my sin to you, nor can you cleanse my soul. Oh, Mundo Cani, Mundo Cani."

Well, the Weasel has had just about enough of this. He thrusts his arms into the Hound's eye sockets, runs out of the chamber and pitches the skull as far as he can. It bounces and rolls and stops.

Now the Rooster is aroused.

"Bring that back!"

"Roostie-riddle, come and get it!" John kicks the skull like a ball, kicks it into the nether-tunnel. Need it be said that John does what he does for the love of his Rooster?

Chauntecleer breathes fury. "Sacrilege!" he screams.

"Prove it, Roostie-riddle! Fight a Douoble-u to gets it back!" John keeps kicking the skull ahead of him, up the marble tunnel.

Now he can hear Chauntecleer coming behind. He takes a quick glance backward. The Rooster's wings are slopping on the ground. Their oils have rendered him flightless. John Wesley has the advantage.

[Twenty-Three]
Oh, Benoni

The first to emerge from the throat of the underworld, the first to gain the shelf at Rachel's den is John Wesley Weasel.

"Inside, Coyote's! John, he's gots the Rooster at his back!"

"Twill! Hopsacking do what the Weasel asks!"

They do, backing into the den. Rachel herself stands guard.

"Benoni," she says. "You too."

But Benoni hesitates.

"Rooster! He's not happy!"

John races down the steps to the stones below. Black-Pale stands as he stood when Chauntecleer first marched through the portal to do battle.

The Weasel pleads with him, "Is not good the Stag, he stays here. Up, Stag! And out!!"

Black-Pale gives no sign that he has heard. He stands unmoved.

"Please, please, please, pretty Stag! Is a Rooster coming!"

Failing to persuade Black-Pale, John rushes up again.

It isn't more than a minute when the Weasel and Rachel and Benoni hear a mighty bugling below.

Then, galloping up the steps of the defile, there come the

second two Creatures out of darkness. Chauntecleer rides the Stag's neck. His weapons, his spurs both Gaff and the Slasher, rake Black-Pale's flesh. John Wesley shrinks from an angry crow, "I am for you, John Wesley!"

Benoni cries, "Do and do for *you!*" He steps off the shelf and begins to descend the steps.

Black-Pale's tongue is thrust out between his teeth. His head is thrown back, his nose in the air. With his antlers he is trying to unseat the Rooster. He does not see where he's going.

Benoni cries, "Do for you!"

Rachel races down to Benoni in order to bring him back.

Then the Stag's right fore-hoof comes down on the young Coyote, snapping his spine. The little Coyote falls several steps lower then lies still as if he were sleeping.

His mother wails, "Benoni! Oh, Benoni!" then throws herself over the ledge. The Stag's hooves trample her too. Then she lies beside her son, licking his face. There isn't a mark on him. But the small Coyote is dead. Then Rachel, his mother, sighs and gives up her ghost.

Running the tundra, Black-Pale-On-A-Silver-Field manages finally to dislodge the Rooster.

[Twenty-Four]
Pertelote at the Sea

"And why mayn't Chalcedony bear a child as Hens do? As any Hen might?"

In the evening before he had departed the Hemlock with the glorious Lord Chauntecleer as the crown in his antlers, Black-Pale-on-a-Silver-Field knelt before his daughter. He nuzzled her for affection and farewell.

De La Coeur had whispered, "Papa, who will watch over me when you are gone?"

The Fawn had regained her health. Her coat was smooth. And bright were her large, liquid eyes.

"Those who have nursed you," her father answered. "They have been kind souls, every one."

Sitting close to this darling family was the Hen Chalcedony. Though Pertelote had ministered most the ailing De La Coeur, it was Chalcedony who had sat by the Fawn all the days and all the nights of her convalescence.

Now she thought to herself, *Why mayn't Chalcedony be the one, she as loves the precious bairn and kissed clean her rheumy eye—?*

The skinny Hen clapped her beak closed, for she realized that she'd spoken her wishes out loud. Chalcedony shrank back, burning with embarrassment.

But Black-Pale swung his head in her direction, his sixteen-point antlers limning arabesques against the dusk.

"Beg pardon, sir, oh sir," she clucked a cluck of shame. "'Twas but a slip of the tongue. 'Twas a pure perversity."

But the Stag kept considering the Hen. Then he said, "Thou?"

The Fawn De La Coeur said, "She tells me the tales that make me sleep, Papa. And I dream good endings for the stories."

"Aye," the Stag said after a moment, "Thou." His voice was royal, but the Hen did not recoil because of his next words: "You shall have a father's lasting gratitude if you consent to befriend my daughter till I come home again."

And so it had been arranged. For a time (and maybe, please, a longer time?), the anemic Chalcedony had her child.

But the child's father never came home again.

Pertelote had never doubted that her husband must spend days accomplishing his mission. Yet, two weeks were almost more than she could bear. It wasn't only that she missed him now. She had been missing him ever since he'd lost sight in one eye and had withdrawn into mystery. And Chauntecleer had taken his challenge to Wyrm as a Rooster crippled.

Two weeks. But Pertelote's distress made it seem a month.

She couldn't sleep. She spent the midnight hours awake on her roost, watching the Beetle Lazara doing her slow duty below, playing the part of a Dung Beetle.

Lazara wore a black babushka and black coverlets over her softer parts. From dusk to dawn she shaped the Animal's waste into balls three times her size, then rolled them with her backward with her back legs to the woods. She who had been capable of digging through stone she dug through the iron of Fimbul-winter to bury the Animals' dreck.

Pertelote took some comfort from her sister's presence.

On the dot of every midnight the cowled Beetled paused and said, "My Lady."

And the Hen answered with the same grave formality, "My Lady."

Each kept company with the other.

But by the sixteenth night Pertelote could no longer give herself over to her wasting apprehension. She had been measuring the stockpiles of food, how quickly they were diminishing. On that sixteenth night the Hen was hectored by a waking dream in which the apparition of her agate-eyed husband stood on the wind. His expression was dead-dull. His coral comb had become a grey slug.

At midnight Lazara said: "My Lady."

Lady! The title scathed Pertelote's spirit. She opened her wings and sank softly to the ground then crept from the Hemlock into the rigid winter. She flew south, the direction her husband had gone on his nighttime flights.

In time a ghostly light presented itself above the southern horizon. Flying closer, Pertelote saw that the glowing exhalations hovered over the length and breadth of a great black island, a *floating* island, so it seemed, because its surface heaved with every heave of the ocean's waves.

Chauntecleer! Is *this* the sea? Is *this* the source of your "wisdom?"

If Fimbul-winter could possibly have gradations, here it seemed more paralyzing than anywhere near the Hemlock.

Coldness of *the* Cold. Darkness of *the* Dark. The dyings

of Death itself.

Yet even under the bitterest conditions the Animals were able to survive since adversity strengthened love, and calamity tightened the bonds among them. But Pertelote feared that it was survival itself that Wickedness sought to shred—by shredding the bonds of love. Therefore, new fears heaped upon old fears. Pertelote thought that neither famine nor the Fimbul-winter were the worst disasters about to befall the Animals.

Where, exactly, where had Chauntecleer gone? Where was this tunnel through which Chauntecleer meant to brave great Wyrm in his dungeons? And how did he hope to defeat Hatred with but two weapons?

He had chosen to characterize himself as Grandeur after Glory. Oh, God, would that this were true.

But Pertelote, trust your husband. He *has* done great things in the past. Can't the fault be yours? Haven't you woven a cloak of your own suspicions? Wait upon him. Trust him as much as you have always loved him. It was he who took you into his community, he who married you, he with whom you bore your children.

Chauntecleer, come home again. I need no victory to honor you. Exhausted, come home again. Defeated, come home again.

Unto his spirit, unto herself, now sitting on the battlefield, Pertelote began to sing:

> "My Lord, what is
>   This poor world's blisse,
> That changeth as the moon?
>   That winter's day
>   You went away
> Was blacked before the noon.

I heard you say,
'Farwell. Oh, nay!
Depart me not so soon.

Why said ye so?
Where did ye go?
Alas! What have ye done?
My weal is woe.
He cannot know
Who loveth two, not one.
Thou hast bestowed
Upon my soul
The wimple of a nun—"

Suddenly Pertelote stopped the song and listened. She heard something like ice grinding between herself and the sea.

Next the wind blew from the waters a loathsome odor. Pertelote gagged. She turned aside and retched.

Again, louder, came that rasping on ice—no, on stone! Then the stone fractured and cracked like a gunshot.

Pertelote ducked. She peeped across the ground. Shards of stone clattered backward through a Beast's hind legs. A Beast of outlandish proportions. Large. He was fifty pounds large, with massive forepaws, legs long and thick with fur, a voluminous bush of a tail, and a mini-sized head!

Pertelote breathed the name of the Beast's race: "Wolverine."

Larcenous Wolverines who prowled only in the dark of night, never letting himself to be seen. At the least little noise, these Creatures would dissolve, as agile as a shadow.

Because the Animals had ever only knew the fetid Wolverine's stink, they called him, "Mr. Fart."

Now, among the shards of stone, Pertelote saw the

silhouette of a small bone spinning away. Then another. Then the Wolverine pulled back from the cavity with rib bones in his jaws. These he broke in a single bite and swilled their marrow. The Woverine rammed his snout into the cavity and brought up a skull.

Pertelote whispered, "Russel, my Fox of Good Sense." And the Wolverine vanished.

[Twenty-Five]
In Which the Weasel Considers Endings

It has always been an article of John Wesley's faith that "Thinkings buggars a blaggard's brains." Nevertheless, here is the Weasel—thinking.

For the first time in his life the Weasel met an ending.

He stands beside the poor Woodie Coyote, both of them staring at the corpses of a mama and her son, and John was filled with mighty emotions. They drove him up and out of the rocky defile and sent him racing across the tundra, following a bloody trail. Maybe he would catch up and fight the Rooster himself. Maybe he would curse the murderous Rooster.

Instead, the Weasel finds Black-Pale returning alone.

"Oh, Stag," says John.

Black-Pale is weary, the sides of his neck slashed.

"Stag?" John repeats as the Stag approaches him then passes him by. The noble Deer walks with his head hung low. He is doubling the bloody tracks of his going—and keeps going until he is out of sight.

The Weasel's bowels twist into a knot: rage and pity and

hysteria. He leaves Black-Pale and bullets the freezing red trail after Chauntecleer.

But the blood ran out before the Rooster is found.

John keeps running, but hopelessly. Finally he loses purpose altogether, and here now he sits—thinking. He is meditating on endings. This grim wilderness seems to be the end of the earth. No bush, no hummock, no outcropping rock, not so much as a ridge of ice to break the visible reaches of the wasteland.

Endings, for there are only so many Critters left on earth, and few at that.

Endings: one by one the Critters will perish. Could be *all* the Critters would die. Then the stars would turn and turn silently—no eyes to see them, nor no voices to cry out.

John Wesley shrivels. Finally his own little life would wink out and then the universe would be deserted altogether, wind and stone and the ice alone.

"Hey! Ho!" The Weasel tries to make the phrase a shout. "Double-u's gives your butts a hundred cuts." Then he says, apropos of nothing, "Please pass the sugar, yo!"

No good. His taunt is a mere puff in his mouth, blowing feathers.

Endings.

[Twenty-Six]
In Which a Daughter
Begins to Grieve

The Fawn De La Coeur raised her head. She opened her nose and sniffed the wind.

"Papa?"

She stood up and walked across the great hall of the Hemlock. She paused a moment, then went out through the silvery boughs and into the brittle weather.

"Papa? Papa?"

Chalcedony rose and flapped her wings and tumble-flew after her ward.

De La Coeur was trotting toward the woods.

"O best beloved," Chalcedony called. "'Tis a troublous thing, to go alone."

But the Fawn out-walked the frail Hen and disappeared among the trees.

Chalcedony pushed her poor self forward. "Ma'am?" she cried back to the Hemlock, "help me! My bairn's gone barmy!"

Then she too was breasting the prickly briars at the edge of the woods. Chalcedony's head had been picked bald. Her feathers gave no protection against the thorns. But what was that when her charge had lost all sense and was endangering herself? And if she, Chalcedony should catch caught up to De La Coeur, what would she do then? Weakness chasing weakness.

Then Chalcedony heard her Fawn's voice, pleading, "Where is my papa? When is he coming home?"

De La Coeur stopped, her nostrils flaring. The words came all from one place. The skinny Hen, gasping at she stumbled around a last tree trunk, saw Creature beside De La Coeur. It was he that she was questioning, "What have you done with my papa?"

John Wesley Weasel. It had been his that the Fawn had smelled. John sat in misery, shaking his head.

He said, "Oh, poor, poor little daughter, your papa—he is hurt. John, he saw his body-hurts. John thinks, might-be his heart is hurt. Oh, little girl. John thinks your papa, he is not coming back. Is two Coyotes killed." John's voice was thick with misery. "Kicked dead," he said. "Not saying the who nor the what did kick them dead. Sad, sad, sad news. By-cause…." John cannot finish the sentence.

De La Coeur began to cry.

[Twenty-Seven]
A Torpor of Guilt

Ferric Coyote has fallen into a deep, reproachful sleep.

"Reproachful" because this is the first thing he did after suffering the sight of his wife's and his son's tortured bodies. Horror kept him from touching their corpses. Horror dizzied him. Suddenly he could not hold his water. Wetness puddled the stones beneath him.

Finally horror drove the hyper-strung Coyote out of the defile, onto the blank tundra. And now, in spite of all, he has fallen asleep.

Ferric refuses to wake. If he did wake up, he would have to endure impossible desolations. O God! What Ferric has feared for most of his life, it has happened. In the end wasn't able to protect his Rachel. He proved himself inadequate. Those he loves have perished. Ferric has become a wretch he cannot look upon.

So: sleep.

But in his sleep he dreams what in fact he saw and heard: the *Tock* of a Stag's hoof. *Tock, tock,* the hoof-sounds descending the rocky defile. And then other sounds: a *Huff-huffing,* and then the bugling of despair.

Ferric dreams that the Stag is whacking his antlers against the stone wall. The tines splinter and crack. Then the great Stag delivers such a hit to the wall that one entire antler breaks from his head, like a timber axed. The hole that was made now begins to bubble blood. Black-Pale collapses. He releases one final, receding sigh and then he too breathes no more.

Ferric dreams another sound: *Yip, yip! Papa!*

The poor Coyote, fearing to dream a dream of his daughters, burrows deeper into his torpor, until he is hiding so profoundly that he becomes a nothing in a nowhere.

[Twenty-Eight]
Pertelote's Sorrow-Song

The Wolves pad softly through the woods, drawn by the coppery scent of blood. Their tongues loll. Their jowls drip saliva.

The White Wolf leads the other two. Therefore, he is first to see the commotion ahead and the first to halt.

A foolish little Hen clucks encouragement. A listless Fawnis weeping. The Hen begs, "Come, child. Dasn't remain. Oh, come with Chalcedony, and take your rest under the Hemlock."

A Weasel seems to be floating away without the benefit of feet.

"Oh," said Boreas, understanding.

It is a wide carpet of Black Ants that carry the Weasel bodily away. And a Hen with browning feathers at her thoat follows them, funereal.

The Hen pauses and turns, and the White Wolf is seen.

"Boreas?" she says.

The White Wolf tingles, so to be found out and named.

The Hen says, "None of you should roam the hinterlands alone. Come. It would not be wrong to walk with me.

There is room."

Nota and Eurus retreat into the shadows.

Boreas murmurs, "Room. But I think there are too many Creatures for our liking."

He thinks that he has spoken privately.

But the Hen hears him. "As you please," she says, then spreads her gracious wings and sails away.

Pertelote has seen the Wolves' eyes as three pairs of lanterns: one pair white, another fire-red, and the third pair as yellow as Wasps.

When the Fawn De La Coeur returns to the hall of the Hemlock, the entire community is borne down by her mood. They close their mouths and walk softly. Mourning requires respect.

The Fawn brings the taint of death.

Then comes John Wesley home again, wounded and dispirited. Those who ask after Chauntecleer, those who want to know how the mission was concluded, receive no answer. It wasn't that the Weasel refuses to answer. Rather, he is as hollow as an Eagle-bone whistle. The Animals have only the Weasel's body by which to reckon events. And this is torn, the eyes barren. Clearly, John Wesley has not returned triumphant.

"Step-Papa?" The Brothers Mice pat John's back. "We are happy to see you. Aren't you happy too?"

But all his fur from the neck to his tail is a tangled mess. Little Mouse-claws cannot comb it clean again.

The entire community loses strength. Tasks are left unfinished. Foodstuffs are only half-eaten. Good relationships dissolve.

Pertelote does her best to provide some hope.

She walks among the Animals singing their names.

"Ratotosk. String Jack. Honey-Queen and your Family

Swarm! Tick-Tock. The Mad House of Otter." And, outside of the Hemlock hall she says to one Ewe Sheep, "Baby Blue!"

Oh, Pertelote wears herself out, trying to lift the spirits of her benumbed community.

And wears herself out the more because she cannot know the state of her husband. John Wesley's condition has destroyed her last shred of confidence. All her guessings lead only to calamity.

So her worries concerning the Rooster are fast becoming anger. Who does he think he is, abandoning his Animals? It never *was* his calling to save the world. Save *these*, Chauntecleer! For *this* were you appointed by the Creator. Save the Keepers who save the world Wickedness and Hatred. Maintain *their* unity.

Oh, the proud fool, off to make himself a her, but reducing the divine "We" to one only: He!

Chauntecleer, Chauntecleer, why do you not come home again?

Oh, how Pertelote yearns to gather the Animals like Chicks under her wings.

And so it was that in the wee hours of the morning, the Hen begins to sing a sorrow-song:

> *"For safety I commend my friends,*
> *Their spirits, sleep, and all their ends*
>   *To God.*
> *And he whose life myself I live,*
> *His name Sweet Singer, most I give*
>   *To God."*

[Twenty-Nine]
Nourishment

Ferric Coyote may have slept for a month, or else for one fathomless night. He slept in a place of no time, and in a time of no place.

And then he wakes to find himself drinking a rich milk.

A low voice says, "Your children, Ferric."

The Coyote opens his eyes. A dun-colored bulk overspreads his vision. Ferric's snout is straight up. When he is able to focus, he realizes that he has been drawing milk from a soft, consoling udder.

At once he jumps backward and begins to shake his head as if he's just pulled it out of a pool of water.

Ferric realizes that he is being watched. Brown eyes, compassionate eyes; a brow furrowed with the truth of the Coyote's grief; nostrils that breathe forth the scent of sweet timothy and a motherly cud; one rangy horn that sweeps the air like a scythe—and the entire Cow covered with a coat the color of dun.

The causes of his grief exist in her as well, but her aspect does not judge him. His mourning has become her mourning, and her lowing gives voice to his heart's inarticulate pain. They

151

grieve together. The reproach that sent him to sleep she has taken into herself, and the water than spills from her eyes may be tears of suffering, or the tears of a heavy repentance.

Now the Cow begins with her tongue to wash the Coyote. And finally he, too, begins to weep.

The Cow lows, "Twill." And she lows, "Hopsacking." And then she drifts away.

Ferric knows. He has been given a job to do. Two jobs, as he understands it.

First he betakes himself to the ledge outside their den. He enters and finds his daughters lying pressed together as if sleeping. But they are not sleeping. They are starving.

He nuzzles them. They both speak with scarcely enough strength to add thanksgiving to their words. "Papa. Here you are."

Ferric says, "I know where food is. I will take you to the food."

His second job is the weightier one.

The rust-red Coyote walks down the steps, half-way to the stones below. His wife and his son should have appropriate graves.

But when he has descended to the level where he last saw them, he finds that the grievous deed has already been accomplished.

Who?

There are three vaults in the wall, each one sealed with a well-cut, elaborate stone door.

And upon the doors have been carved three names.

"Rest in peace, Rachel Coyote."

"Rest in peace, Benoni Coyote."

"Rest in peace, Black-Pale-on-a-Silver-Field."

Who?

Ferric smells the scent of sweet timothy and a benevolent cud.

So, then: interment was not necessary. It is mercy. It is the shriving of all his iniquities.

[Thirty]
A legend

In the ancient ages there was a Creature named Leviathan who sported in the ocean waters. Eyes lidded had the Creature, like the closings of the day. His breath could kindle coals on the surface of the waters. His heart was as hard as a millstone. And when the behemoth swam, he left a hoary wake behind him.

Once, so the legend goes, a flock of Swans, wearied by their long migrations, spied an island midway between the northern shores and the southern shores of the global ocean. It was a bald land. It offered nothing more than a place to rest. The sea was too briny for the oils in their feathers which kept them afloat, for it dissolvedthe oils and soaked their plumage, bidding fair to drown the great Birds. Therefore, they were forced land and to rest on that island.

After the Swans had regained strength, they flew on, telling every ocean-going Bird of the island in the middle of the sea.

Through the years that followed, then, generations of itinerate Birds took advantage of the dry ground. Their guano piled up. Seeds in the guano germinated and sprouted. Grasses and reeds, bushes and, finally, small trees graced its land .

Why, the Birds asked themselves, should we leave this so

fruitful an island?

So they spend their broody seasons right where they nest and hatched their helpless chicks, feeding them until they were fully fledged and able to fly.

They came and they stayed.

Ants arrived. Butterflies, Bugs, Beetles, and soon a goodly society populated the place. Peace prevailed. They did not hurt nor destroy on all this holy, oval land.

But then, in the perfect month of Creaturely fellowship, when Chicks could cheep but could not fly, the entire island rose up, seawater sluicing down its sides, tsunamis rolling like foothills in ever widening circles. For from the beginning the island had been the monster Leviathan.

And now Leviathan, wearing the green and breathing laurels of victory, plunged down into the deeps.

And they, good Creatures all, drowned.

[Thirty-One]
Home Again

Chauntecleer's return was inauspicious. He came soundlessly in the night. The wakeful Pertelote heard a small *Tink* outside the Hemlock. With the second *Tink* she knew its source. It was the tip of a spur touching ice.

Chauntecleer!

She wanted her husband all to herself. Therefore she muffled her flight like the wings of Owls and went out to meet him.

"Chauntecleer?"

He stood stupidly, avoiding her eyes. When she reached for him, he moved away.

"My Lord?"

He turned his back.

Even in the darkness she saw that his pearl eye was gone. Pertelote could see this because something else was glowing amber in the socket. And look: something amber was hanging from his nostrils. Chauntecleer shook his head: *Get away from me.* And amber tendrils dropped to the ground.

Pertelote felt a kind of horror, watching the ghastly discharge.

"Chauntecleer? Won't you speak to me?"

He shook his head, *No.*

"Please tell me what happened to you."

No.

"I will give you my heart, if it could heal you."

But the Rooster began heavily to move toward the Hemlock. He could not so much as raise his head. He was fat with grease.

So then: the world was lost. All the Creatures were all lost if Chauntecleer had lost bravura.

Oh, my soul, what sadness has come upon us now?

So the Rooster had come home. Hope was extinguished. He spent his days and his nights crouched of his roosting limb.

The Black Ants grew aggravated. Dizziness *ain't work, sir! Blast you for your—oh shit. Forget it.*

Pertinax Cobb chose to keep inside his burrow.

"This time, Mrs. Cobb, I don't mind saying: I *am* complaining."

"This time you have every right."

"The dismal Rooster makes a powerful stink."

"Mr. Cobb, you speak my very thoughts."

Mrs. Cobb said, "The stink could suffocate an unwary Squirrel."

"Indeed."

"No need to share our food no more."

"You are a thoughty one, Mr. Cobb."

"They *pee* on food, the stupid Animals."

Even Pertelote had no will for housecleaning, nor the strength for song. Her single consolation was the abiding Beetle, Lazara.

"My Lady."

"My Lady."

Nothing deterred the Dung Beetle from her duty. The floor of the hall might be covered in a thick mat of waste. The smell might burn Pertelote's eyes. But Lazara never protested. Devoutly she rolled it all into balls and rolled the balls away.

The Brothers Mice, on the other hand, did not doubt the possibilities of healing. They loved their Rooster. They believed that laughter could lighten the deepest darkness.

There came the day, then, when Chauntecleer developed a double—a tiny self behind himself.

For here came Freitag, hopping like a Bird on two legs, his forepaws clasped behind his back, his little face scrunched into the lines of desolation.

The big Cock stepped. The little one stepped.

In circles went Chauntecleer. In circles, Freitag.

"Hum," said the Mouse, overcome with melancholia. "Hum, hum, hum."

Suddenly six more Mice lined up in front of Chauntecleer intended to go. They began to clap.

Chauntecleer stepped over them. So they ran ahead and lined up again. "Look," they cried. "Watch Freitag, dear Chanty-cleer."

Again the Rooster stepped over the line of Mice. Again they scrambled forward and lined up directly in his way. Samstag jumped up and kissed the Rooster on his beak.

Chauntecleer stopped. He blinked. The Mice cried, "Hoorah!" and Freitag commenced the best part of his act.

"Heh," he said. This was a sigh. He mopped his face and rolled his eyes to the skies and said: "Oh, 'tis a monumental sad thing, to be alive."

Freitag folded his paws and began to pray: "If only a body could walk the world another way than alive! Heh and heh, and mercy me."

The little Mouse bent down and delivered a truly tragic moan, moaned until there wasn't another scrap of air left in his tiny lungs, and, the best thespian of the seven Mice, looked crushed by misery.

Well! Then his brothers broke into a wild applause. "You got him, Freitag! You got him to a T!"

Freitag began to pump his small head up and down. In perfect solemnity he spun both forelegs like propellers. He leaned back and opened his mouth, and his brothers cried: "It's Chanty-cleer! It's Chanty-cleer, getting ready to crow!"

Freitag made a *Crick* sound, then yelled, "Stop, sun! Halt, moon! Don't none of you clouds go potty on me. I'm gonna tell you of times and the time!"

Then, throwing back his head the Mouse crowed:

> *"Kicky-kee-diddle-dee-dee!*
> *I make the laws up for ye!*
> *And here's the main one*
> *To kicky your bum:*
> *Shut up! And leave-a-me be!"*

Oh, what a crow! Straight from the good old days!

The Brothers beat each others' backs and roared with laughter until they collapsed, tears of happiness running from their eyes. They beeped and blew their noses.

"Oh," they sobbed. "Oh, dear Rooster, wasn't that the most wonderfulest thing?"

But Chauntecleer stepped over them all as if nothing had happened, and walked away.

He left the Mice feeling ashamed.

Freitag, little Freitag, their second youngest Brother, fought with all his might to keep his lower lip from trembling.

• • •

That night Chauntecleer returned to his roost and took his place by Pertelote. She could not bring herself to be grateful, yet she chose to stay beside him. He did not touch her, nor was there warmth in his body. There were, instead, those incomprehensible worms.

But he spoke.

"No one," he said as if to no one, "knows failure as I know failure now."

And that was all he said, and she suffered his cold silence.

Watch Lazara. Try to take comfort in Lazara.

"My Lady," the Beetle said on the tick of midnight.

But tonight Pertelote could not respond.

Come morning and Chauntecleer heard the Hens cackling, *fighting* together. Their cries grew louder and angrier Chauntecleer dropped to the ground.

He landed poorly. His first steps faltered.

The Hens had formed a nattering circle. Inside it two Hens raced at breakneck speeds, one chasing the other. Fat Jasper nipped at Chalcedony's heels. When Chalcedony tried to break through the circle, her sister caught her and pitched her back at Jasper.

Immediately Jasper leaped onto Chalcedony's back. Jasper forced the skinny Hen to lie flat on the ground. Then began to peck the flesh behind her comb. The pink skin was already freckled with old scabs. Jasper was biting new wounds, her furious beak pinking Chalcedony's skull with blood.

Chauntecleer roared, "By God, stop this!"

The whole community was stunned. For an instant *everything* stopped. The Hen's circle fractured.

Chauntecleer hissed, "Jassss-per."

The fat Hen jumped up. She ruffled her feathers and puffed her wattles with contempt and superiority. A hiss for a hiss: Jasper spat, "Not my fault!"

"Whose fault then?"

Jasper aimed a fat claw backward. "Hers! The rag that's lying there! Her that took it on the lam soon's the war was over. Pretending to be a *dead*, miss Good-for-Nothing, is what *I* say."

Chauntecleer whispered: "Started what?"

"Stealing food."

"The rule is, Share."

"Don't I know it! And you, bleeding itty bitty pary-sites! Mealy worms crawling in great Lord Rooster's brains!"

Chauntecleer raised a wing. Jasper ducked. But he only meant to cover his hollow socket.

That duck on Jasper's part, that compulsive defense increased the fat Hen's indignation. "Mister Cock-of-the-Poop-Walk," she snapped. "Hey, Mister Piss! You gonna come and tell *us* the rules?"

She aimed a savage peck at his head. "Mister Fake! You *cancel* rules!"

Then, forlornly, Chauntecleer stumbled out of the Hemlock hall.

Now Pertelote flew from her roost and swooped at the Fat Hen. Pertelote's claws became deadly weapons. She slashed the back of Jasper's neck, then ripped the feathers out by their roots. But then Pertelote too sank to the ground. The fight went out of her. For she saw an amber maggot sticking to Jasper's tongue. The fat Hen closed her beak and swallowed the maggot down.

Chauntecleer had gone to seek sympathy from the sea.

Once before its rolling breakers had thundered the

rhythms that eased him. Father ocean. Booming lullabies. Oh, receive me now, and I will never leave you again.

His legs ached. His wings drooped. His toes were crooked. His walk was crippled. His feathers were oily. They could not keep out the cold.

Where else could he go but to Wyrmesmere?

Prop me up, great sea. Prop me up in all my leaning places.

He stopped and cocked his good eye forward. The ground had been disturbed. The Rooster saw distinctly a rupture on the battlefield.

"Oh, no."

His heart began to beat. Emotion arose within him. He raised his head on a long stalk and peered at the ravaged earth.

"No!" he snarled. "Not that!"

Chauntecleer's legs were empowered by a fresh vexation. He ran. For he had seen that Russel's grave had been destroyed!

Damn it! Bones and Fox teeth lay scattered about. A thighbone had been cracked and the marrow sucked out of it. And water swirled in the bottom of the hole that Lazara had digged.

"Wyrm!" screamed Chauntecleer.

He opened his wings and flew, unaware of his renewed strength. Rage enabled him. He stroked the air across the wide, lifeless scar, then landed on the white salt beaches of the sea.

"Wyrm! Bastard! What have you done?" Wyrm was dead. But his mind must be alive!

[Thirty-Two]
An Experiment in Climbing

Pertelote, weary and eternally awake on her roost, heard small scratchings at the base of the Hemlock. Then she heard Mouse-whisperings, tiny calculations like thieves preparing a raid.

It was night. What she saw below looked like nothing so much as purposeful hair-balls, yet she recognized Wodenstag by his manner and Donnerstag by his leadership.

Six of the Brothers stood semi-circle, staring straight up with their mouths hanging open, while the seventh, Wodenstag, began to climb the tree's trunk. All four of his little limbs were extended as wide as they could no. He was a daddy-longlegs clinging to the bark. And he was trembling so violently that he looked like a plucked rubber band. Yet his expression was earnest, and somewhere inside of him was the conviction that a Mouse could climb a tree.

The Brothers whispered, and Pertelote heard them whispering, "Are you going to fall, Wodenstag? Should we get out of the way?"

By a grand effort the mighty Wodenstag stuck to the trunk. He chin was drumming it like a woodpecker—and lo! His eyes lit up. It must have been the chin-drumming that presented him with a solution for climbing better, for he whispered to his Brothers, "Bite the bark." Six Mice cheered scarcely audible cheers. ("Hoo-ray.")

Wodenstag planted his teeth in a bit of wood, which allowed him to reach higher and grab new bark with the nails of his paws. Up a step, up a step.

Six Brothers began to attempt the climb themselves, making a constant buzzing of grunts. A string of thieves up a tree. And how they encouraged Samstag, the youngest of them all.

One by one they gained a tough limb above. Whisperingly they congratulated Samstag when he arrived beside them. In unison then they turned and looked down the limb to the Lady Hen who was roosting maybe ten feet away.

"Shhh," said Wodenstag. "Shouldn't wake her."

Pertelote experienced a true consolation. Of all the Creatures it was the Brothers Mice who remembered kindness.

Then here came brave Wodenstag, balancing along the limb, picking his inches with monumental care. After him came Donnerstag, frowning severely. And Sonntag, and so forth, all staring at the precious limb as if to stare was to grip.

Then this is what they did: they lined up next to Pertelote side by side, sitting on two legs—which was the peril, sitting on two legs only.

Independently of one another, the Mice began to rock. Forward and backward like round-bottomed pepper shakers. Too far forward ("Whoa!"), too far backward ("Whoa! Whoa!), but all with the greatest solemnity and an air that it was proper to be right here, that there was no other place to be, Amen.

Pertelote, the Hen for whom they came, felt a pressure in her breast which might have been laughter, or it might have been sobbing, either one.

"'Tags," she whispered.

"Ah, Lady, we didn't mean to wake you up. Wodenstag began to pat her wing.

"But you are here."

"Yes. All of us, one, two, six, seven."

"Whoa!" said Samstag. Then Freitag said, "Whoa!" spinning his forelegs like whirligigs.

"A very hard thing," said Pertelote, "to climb a tree."

"But we," said Wondenstag, "tricked it."

"Whoa!" cried Dienstag, and he fell of the limb.

Pertelote said, "I don't suppose it's easy for a Mouse to sit this way."

"Roosting," said Wodenstag.

And Pertelote said, "Roosting."

"Whoa!" One by one the Brothers dropped.

Wodnstag said, "But we agreed that this would be an excellent wasy to sleep sometimes."

Plop, plop, plop. Mice hit the ground. And *Plop*—Wodenstag might have followed, except that he grabbed a Pertelote-feather and dangled over emptiness.

"So," he said, "we said, 'We should keep the Lady company.' We have us, but you have nobody."

Pertelote sobbed. It was *both* laughter *and* tears inside her breast. The sob felt very good, but it did no good for Wodenstag, who lost his grip and dropped right past Diestag, already on his way up the trunk again.

"The carefulest," Pertelote sighed, "and the kindest friends I know."

She spread her wings and sank to the ground. Instantly every Mouse that was ascending became Mice descending.

Pertelote said, "Do you think that we could all sleep on the ground tonight?"

Wodenstag said, "A very fine idea."

Soon, under her wings, seven separate paws were patting the down upon her breast.

And Pertelote sang, as if her husband had come and were sitting beside them all.

> "Chauntecleer, remember laughter.
> Chauntecleer, let your long langour
>   Cease.
> O Chauntecleer, your Creatures weep.
> They beg you Crow and you safekeep
>   Them each."

[Thirty-Three]
Warriors! Armies! Death to Surt on her Island!

At the first flush of the dawn a mighty Lauds, a brassy reveille went far and wide across the land.

The Animals gaped into wakefulness.

Lord Chauntecleer was crowing from the topmost crown of the Hemlock tree.

"Get up!" he crowed." We have a war to wage!"

Even the Wolves and the Marten Selkirk responded, so absolute was the command.

Chauntecleer's substance had swelled. His hackles, his cape, the feathers on his back showed muscles rolling underneath.

"My Creatures! Gather as armies before me!"

Pertinax Cobb stiffened.

"Pack up, Mrs. Cobb."

"Why, Mr. Cobb?"

"I am a peaceful Squirrel."

"None more peaceful than you."

"Armies, Mrs. Cobb. Warfare. I don't like warfare."

Still as a golden flag above the, Chauntecleer the Rooster thrashed his wings. "We cannot wait. Wickedness blows abroad. Once more, one last time more, we must assault the pernicious presence."

Pertelote was blindsided. Chauntecleer had returned to his old power. But there was no joy in it. His dominance quivered with something like wrath. And the amber worms? She saw none of them. On the other hand, she *did* see something like smoke blasting from his throat. It was as if his words were visible.

The Animals dithered in confusion.

"There is an island in the sea to the south. Flames dance its surface. Fire that turns the ocean and he sky above it lurid. And Surt is that fire! But Surt, I swear, *is* the fire! And Surt is the off-scourings of the body of Wyrm! Therefore, Surt is wickedness of Wickedness, and the hatreds of Hate. It is a crusade! It shall be a holy war! Armies upon armies, who will go with me?"

Apparently, no one. Animals heard Lord Chauntecleer's commanding voice and were troubled—both by the fear of slaughter *and* by the ineluctable manner of the Rooster on his pinnacle. They had loved him. But this was an iron Bird, a Vulture with talons.

Chauntecleer trebled his volume. "What?" he roared. "Have all your spirits withered? Have you become a weak-kneed rabble? Tick-Tock, reveal yourself."

The Black Ant appeared. "Sir!" He snapped both feelers to attention. His polished eye gleamed.

"Rouse your battalions."

Tick-Tock was by nature a warrior. He pivoted with a military kick. "Battalions! We defeated Wyrm once before. Are you keen to have at him again?"

Regiments of Black Ants massed the ground before their Commander. "Yes *sir!*"

Tick-Tock bellowed, "I can't hear you."

The troops boomed, "Sir! Yes *Sir!*"

Chauntecleer left his perch and sailed above Tick-Tock's regiments, reviewing the thousand boot-black Ants.

"Even so!" he crowed with satisfaction. "Who is next? Who will set their store by me? Rise up, my armies, and march!"

March? Away from the high tower and security?

Pertelote was as transfixed as the rest of the Animals, but more disquieted than they. She had ceased to believe in her husband. March? He was suicidal.

Chauntecleer alighted beside her. "Hen, stir up these mollycoddles! I am boldness itself. If they are not mine they must be yours. "

No, it wasn't smoke that blew from his throat. Specks. A horde of Midges. And less than Midges, they were pinpoint-Insects on the wing.

And what was the Rooster doing now? Heaping mountains onto mountains until their summits breached the heavens.

He flew up and circled, brass-banging the multitude with his crowing. "Those not with me are against me."

The sheer menace in Chauntecleer's threat knocked Ratotosk Bore-Tooth, the Grey Squirrel from his nest. But a Squirrel lands belly-down. He dashed for a root hole at the base of the Hemlock.

Chauntecleer swooped to the woods. He strutted to the three Wolves there.

"Your kind can kill," he declared. "It was one of your grandfathers raped my mother. He killed her, and I killed him. I had that right then, and I have it now. Join me and you shall know my mercy. I want you for my shock troops."

Boreas the White Wolf stood on a rise. Eurus and Nota stood directly in front of the Rooster, Nota glaring with her red eyes. She lowered her head and retracted her lips. This was not submission. Her tail sprang up like a flag.

She growled, "I don't know you. You have no authority over me."

Eurus circled around the Rooster. Each Wolf was thrice his size. These two formed a pincer at his back and his breast.

Chauntecleer dilated his body. "You have no choice," he said in a silk-smooth voice. He bent the knee of one blue leg and with the point of one spur cut a line across the ice. "Submit or I will slash you one by one."

Nota and Eurus answered with rumbling growls.

Chauntecleer crowed, "Behold!" The crow blew a dust of Insects from his throat. He jumped and cut Nota's ear, then whirled and scarred Eurus in the lip. Their tails dropped. They began to rub their eyes, red and yellow. They sneezed and sneezed.

Chauntecleer said, "There they are, my shock troops bowed before me now."

He swung away from the Wolves and flew to the top of a nearby pine.

"Selkirk," he crowed. "I see you. I know where you nest."

The Marten leaped from that pine to another. Chauntecleer was as nimble as he. The instant the Marten caught a new branch, there was a spur full in is face. "Try that once more, and Gaff will scour your skull."

Selkirk froze.

Chauntecleer hissed, "You are my scout. You are my outrider."

He left the Marten, who twisted and bit at the irritations in his anus.

The Rooster dropped and strutted toward the Hemlock. He stopped before the moribund Weasel.

"So," he said. "The bone thief."

John Wesley stood and glowered and said, "Bones is bones. Is a Rooster what steals a *Rooster.*"

Chauntecleer flew to the hive of the Family Swarm, "Queen," he demanded. "Honey Bees all! I want you to be my Killer Bees. Fly south with me."

Then he bore down on the House of Otter. "I need water horses." He thrust his head into their hapless faces. "I want distance swimmers, wet coats and stone slayers." Those infinitesimal Insects blew like wisps to the moisture in the Otters' nostrils and eyes.

Once again, Chauntecleer ascended to his topmost spire. This Cock was nothing like a weather vane. He *was* the weather. And who could endure his eye-beam? His right eye sent forth the torch of a refiner's fire.

"Black Ants, henceforth *Army* Ants! Neither hills nor bodies will obstruct your going. March lockstep south to the sea. At the coastline make mats of yourself. Assemble rafts by which to float to the bonfires on the Island of Surt."

This was a Rooster Pertelote had never seen before. No! She *had* seen one: the reptilian Cockatrice that once had attacked the true Chauntecleer!

"As for the rest of you puling, self-serving varmints," Chauntecleer crowed. "Oh, how I detest betrayal!"

And, on mighty wings, he flew away.

Chauntecleer never again removed his weapons, not until the day he died.

[Thirty-Four]
To Do What Must Be Done

"Bones is bones," John Wesley said.

The Weasel's sadness had resolved itself into a desolation of spirit.

Chauntecleer had berated Pertelote no less than he had the other Animals. His crow had stupefied her. She'd sunk down and covered her head with the feathers of one wing. And so she had stayed for the rest of the day.

And the Rooster had absolutely no call to chide *him*, John Wesley Weasel!

By evening John's emptiness was filled with pity. And pity sent him to Pertelote.

"Lady Hen? Is Lady Hen asleeping?"

"Hush, John. Let the Animals rest."

"Is awake, then?"

"What do you think?"

"Well. Okay. So: wants a Lady Hen, might-be, talk with a Double-u?"

"I am here."

John coughed. It was difficult, this thing he had to say. "Is a puzzlement: a Rooster what is not a Rooster."

Pertelote raised her wing back and looked at the Weasel.

John said, "Listen, Lady Hen. Is a Rooster what is not *the* Rooster. Is a monstrous sad truth John gots a need to tell. Worser and worser and worser."

"What can be worse than what we have already witnessed?"

Before he lost his nerve, the Weasel hurried into his story.

"Rooster, he *is* hate. *Is* Wickedness. Is damn Hell on Critters!"

"Not damned, John!"

"Him what is the Not-Rooster. *That* Rooster. Lady: Was *his* hatefulness what murdered little Coyote Benoni. Murdered his mama too."

"Oh, John, John, don't say so."

" Sad papa. Sad little daughters. Is a Not-Rooster. Might-be is a true Rooster too."

Pertelote was weeping.

"Something is smoldering inside him, John. I've seen the smoke—"

"No! Not smoke! John knows that Lady Hen, she knows same as John. But she don't wants to be knowing."

Pertelote had begun to rock like a child in fear of punishment.

If a Weasel can tame his voice to soothe another, John lowered his and strove for gentleness. "This Double-u," he said. "This Double-u, he loves his Chauntecleer."

Pertelote suffered an explosive sob.

"John goes now, John does the do what he can still do."

When Coyotes howl long, plaintive wailings in the dead of night; when they round their mouths to the sky and utter shrill notes, this is what they are saying:

Son of my sorrow, what has heaven done to you?

They are the Voice, these Coyotes. They are themselves lamentation and bitter weeping. They are weeping for their children. And they cannot be comforted, for their children are not.

This is the way of the world.

Children die.

And when the Hen Pertelote cries in the night, this is what she is saying:

> "That summer's courtship's long gone by,
> Those evenings when my Lord and I
>   Were young.
> Oh, take my tears on faith and I
> Will stroke your neck—my lullabies
>   Unsung."

[Thirty-Five]
Comes Savagery

The eggs had been laid. The incubation of the wispy Insect's maggots lasted but one cryptic hour. And then violence seized the land.

String Jack hop-bounded to Pertelote under the Hemlock, yipping frantically.

"Lady-Lady! Lady-Lady!" His ears popped up *(Bang! Bang!)*, and his round eyes stared in two directions

"Slow down, String Jack. What's the matter?"

"Yep yep." But the Hare sat, perpetually startled.

"Is it too much to say? Say it."

"Yep. Nope nope."

Under other circumstances Perlelote would have read the Hare's hesitation as shyness. But this was anguish. "When you are able, Jack, tell it to me."

"We saw his head!" the Hare cried, nipping his words. *"We"* must mean himself and his relations. "Dead," he cried.

"Jack! *Who* is dead?"

"Dead. All his bones picked clean."

Again Pertelote said, "Slow down." And again, *"Who* is dead?"

"Ratotosk. Boring Tooth. Him. Blood spots under a tree. In the woods, blood spots. We found the head bone." The Hare pointed toward the forest.

Pertelote said, "Show me."

So the Hare led the Hen to a particular pine, and Pertelote whispered, "No."

It was the tree that Selkirk the Marten had made his own. Caught in the fork of a limb was Ratotosk's tail, the bushy fur intact, but the tail itself bitten from its base.

High above her Pertelote heard a swish of branches. Selkirk was leaped from pine to pine, farther and farther away, but Pertelote had glimpsed blood on the Marten's snout.

Suddenly Pertelote's heart turned. She loathed the Hares for their round-eyed timidity. These passive Animals! Docile and witless—a dead weight on her back!

Then to the north she heard a terrified bleating.

Pertelote forgot herself. She flew in the direction of the terror.

Sheep! She saw one Ewe on an eastern hillside, running, stumbling, falling—and the Black Wolf Nota after the Sheep, her eyes inflamed.

With a sixteen-foot bound crashed into the Sheep. He locked his fangs on her windpipe.

Pertelote screamed, "Nota! Let her go!"

But the Black Wolf paid no attention. She held the Ewe's throat until the Creature went limp. Then he shook the body savagely. Blood splattered the earth. The Black Wolf threw her prey aside.

Pertelote was horrified. The Sheep that the Wolf had murdered was Baby Blue.

Now Nota drove her muzzle into Blue's abdomen and began to gorge herself.

Pertelote was transfixed. She whispered, "Oh, Nota, what a Wolf can do."

And how sharp are a Wolf's ears. Black Nota whirled, saw the Hen, lowered her head, and glared at her through manic, blood-red eyes. Foam dripped from the Wolf's jowls. Amber maggots squirmed in the saliva.

Peretelote muted the cry, *My God.*

Nota returned to the Ewe. She sank her fangs in the flesh and dragged out the long rope of intestine, then ran her snout in the steaming carcass, and probed, and pulled out the slick liver, and ate it. She ate as much as twenty pounds, then the wandered into a leafless thicket, slumped, and went to sleep.

Night fell. Pertlote became a pale splash in the moonlight. She crouched right where she was, emptied of all thought.

After she'd spent an hour in the darkness, she chose to believe that her immobility was a midnight vigil.

Someone should sit vigil for the slaughtered Baby Blue.

[Thirty-Six]
A Rachel-Story

When she is tired, the plain Brown Bird rides Ferric Coyote's rump.

He noses the scent of the Weasel, wherefrom he maps their traveling, his and Twill's and Hopsacking's and the Bird herself. No longer does the Coyote hide. It has done no good in the past. It can do no good in the future.

Moreover, he is bolder than he has been. Though Rachel has passed away, her spirit comforts him. He has become the mother of h is daughters.

When the Brown Bird has rested, she leaves Ferric. She cannot sing. She says, "Zicküt," and dances on the wind to keep the grils entertained and to quiet their aching hungers.

At night the Coyotes curl into one another, and Ferric tells them Rachel-stories.

For example:

There is a certain Eagle whose name is Aquila. In time Aquila grows very old. His wings grow slow and heavy. His eyes grow dim in mists of senility. And his whole body becomes infirm and like as not to die. But the Eagle need not die.

For he knows of an oasis in the middle of a desert, a

palmy acre, green and good. In the middle of the oasis is a bright, bracing pool. In the middle of the pool a wonderful fountain shoots up, the top of which falls open like the plume of a lily.

Aquila drinks from the pool and gains strength for a final flight.

He points his beak to heaven and soars as straight as a plumb line from the oasis to the circle of the sun. Higher and at his heighest the sun's rays evaporate the mists in his eyes. Higher still, the sun's flames scorch his feathers to cinders.

So then there is no help for it. He plunges headfirst down from the sun, and down until he falls into the white blossom of the fountain. In that sweet water Aquila is washed as if by honey and wine. Among the green palms he sprouts new feathers that flash in the daylight, and his youth is renewed.

Now Ferric finishes the tale as did his wife before him.

"Rest, my children. God will bless you, and I'll be here in the morning."

[Thirty-Seven]
Sweet Baby Blue and the Fawn De La Coeur

Mr. and Mrs. Cobb decided to make their departure in stages. Pertinax had excellent reasons to leave, and his wife did not disagree. They were a peace-loving folk.

But when two somebodies have lived all their lives in one place, then every other place is strange. Generations of Cobbs had been born here under the Hemlock, had worked here, bore children here, slept their winters here, and died here. And Pertinax's duty had always been to love his wife and to serve her and, upon her love, to bring the next generation onto this same small plot.

How, then, could they go away?

But however could they stay?

They left. They planned to make the emigration in stages. Travel half a day, then sit and test the place. What's the weather? How is the ground? Where are the seeds? Can a new next house and sustain them? Or will the angry Animals spread their wars this far?

If the soil is poor and seeds unplenty, and if warfare creeps too close, they would up and travel another half-day farther.

"Mrs. Cobb?"

"Yes, Mr. Cobb?"

"Are you tired yet?"

"Side by side with you, Mr. Cobb. Side by side wherever we go."

"Well then what do you say? Is this a place to homestead?"

Half a day's travel, at their cautious rate, is half one hundred yards.

And the night, of course, is for sleeping.

When the two of them woke in the morning, Pertinax combed his whiskers, picked food from between his teeth with a twig, and gargled. All this while Mrs. Cobb went off into the bushes to do her business. They had come east, and east she went. Pertinax tried to break ground but the ice prevented him.

"Mr. Cobb," she said, returning, rubbing her nose. "Mr. Cobb, I smell a terrible odor."

"Well," he said, and because they had a stick-to-your-guns sort of marriage, they walked forward, but mincingly.

Indeed. Something before them was rank.

They worked their ways under an ice-tinkling bush and came out the other side where Pertinax's tail sprang straight up. The sight held both him and his wife fast.

For they had known Sweet Baby Blue.

Her eyes were closed; her grey tongue was stuck out and stiff as though beseeching heaven with an unheard cry. Oh, this was all too private. How could friends look on the gnawed-blood-nakedness of a once good friend?

But neither Cobb considered running. Their eyes had shifted to the cavity where her guts had been. Tiny eggs were attached to her interior meat, massed in perfect rows, rows upon rows.

Pertinax took several steps nearer, but then, feeling ghoulish, halted.

He whispered, "Mrs. Cobb, this is wrong."

She whispered, "Poor Baby Blue."

He said, "Yes. What happened to her is wrong. But—"

Under the death odor he'd caught the scent of spite, the treacle of hubris and of Lupine savagery. Pertinax was angry. *Now* he moved, stepping toward the ravaged Baby Blue.

Then a Hen came thrashing through the frozen bushes, swearing. "Chip-shit! Chippy-chippy Chipmunks! Them eggs is mine!"

Jasper the Hen pitched her fat body at Pertinax.

"Mr. Cobb!" shrieked Mrs. Cobb.

The Hen caught Pertinax in her right claw. Four yellow nails encaged him.

Mrs. Cobb wrung her forepaws. She should save her husband. But there were no holes for refuge.

"Feathers and fur," Jasper cackled. "Fur and feathers— and which d'you thinks is prettier, Mister?"

Pertinax determined not to answer, not to beg. He must leave Mrs. Cobb with the memory of a courageous Mr. Cobb.

Jasper screamed, "Which is the prettier, Rat?"

Manfully, Peretinax kept his mouth shut.

"Feathers, Rat-shit! Feathers!"

In her claw Jasper carried Pertinax over to a smooth stone, yelling, "Knock-a-the, knock-a-the, knock-a-the Rat's head *dead!*"

She pinned Pertinax to the ground. She picked up a stone—

Just then another Hen raised a voice as frightening as a siren, "Jasper! For the love of God!"

Pertelote swooped down on the fat Hen, seized her head

in one furious claw, and wrenched it.

Jasper gurgled. She spat out a knot of amber worms, then screamed, "Off-a-me, you Rooster's bitch!" She twisted and bit one of Pertelote's toes. The two Hens fell away from each other. Pertinax Cobb jumped free.

Jasper yelped at the loss of her prisoner.

Pertelote had the clearer mind. She dived at Jasper's, flipped her, and tore at the fat Hen's wattles till they bled.

Jasper shrieked curses. She found her feet and paddled away as fast as her legs could carry her. "See if I don't, Missus," she screeched. "Just *see* if I don't!"

Pertelote lay down and groaned. "I hate this," she sobbed. "I *hate* this."

While the Hen and the two Ground Squirrels were mourning Sweet Baby Blue, the soot-colored Nota prowled west of the Hemlock, hungry again.

Her head slung low between her shoulders, she had tracked the Fawn De La Coeur to this valley. This prey would be an easy catch, for she reclined, having folded her forelegs under her chest, and seemed oblivious, lost in sorrow. A stringy Hen stood by, murmuring words in the Fawn's ear. Nota wondered whether the Hen thought she was guarding the Fawn. If so, she was no more than a trinket constructed of tendons and reeds and not worth the trouble.

All at once the Hen set up a piercing clamor. She ran round and round the Fawn, raising a hell of a squawk. "Wolf," she gabbled. "O Baby get up and go. It's a Wolf in the thicket!"

The Hen's alarum electrified Nota. As a single, taut nerve she broke from cover. Kill that damn Hen? Or skip her and strike the Fawn's tender flesh?

Both!

Nota seized the Hen in her teeth, and whirled her, and slammed her to the ground. Chalcedony managed one pitiful cry, then quivered and went slack.

In the time it took to kill the Hen, the Fawn had leaped to her feet and went bounding, twenty-five feet in a flight.

Nota streaked after her. The wind ripped strings of saliva from her jowls. She had strength and endurance and the rage of a hunter. She would run a mile if she had to, but didn't think she'd have to. The Black Wolf skimmed the ground like an arrow launched. Hunter and hunted performed a *Totentanz*, a mortal dance across the valley.

In half a minute Nota reached the aerial Deer. Nota leaped. She lanced the space between them, almost pouncing on the Fawn's hindquarters—

But then the whole world seemed to slow down, and Nota floated as in a dream.

She heard a specter-like crow: "For your father, child."

Then the crow was close above her: "For your father, too noble for this earth."

The Wolf experienced a clean, painless parting of the artery in her neck. The world turned.

Nota thought, *Am I this child? Am I a child again?*

The ground came up, and her fall came down, and she and the earth met as loves meet. Darkness swaddled her, and Nota never woke to another morning.

In the sound of a whirlwind Lord Chauntecleer swept away.

> Feathers like banners, glorious, golden,
> Upon his frame once floated and flowed.
> (This, all this, was in the olden
> Long-ago.)

And though the golden Lord once dallied
   (In those sweet days)
Around the Hemlock, plumed and grand, he's
   Gone away.

[Thirty-Eight]
All the Dying, All the Dead

The Marten Selkirk has left the Hemlock of his own accord.

The blood which he drank from the veins of Ratotosk the Grey Squirrel congealed in his stomach. Spasms wracked his body. And then the Hen Pertelote arose to damn his carnage, and this, he believes, was the beginning of his punishment.

A part of his soul is riven, for he deserves any punishment to which righteousness condemns him.

But another part of his soul craves slaughter, and more pulsing blood.

He knows not which part will dominate: decency or bestiality.

Therefore, Selkirk roams the frozen wilderness alone.

A mother's children never completely leave her. Not even death is thief enough to destroy their spirits.

Pertelote remembers their burial. Remembers the small tombstones set like dolmens upon their graves. Her children were lost in Wyrm's destructions, but she did not, and does not, rue the loss. The stones are in her bosom now. She bears them lightly. She has herself become her sons' memorial.

But now *this*, Sweet Baby Blue violated. How did the Wolf's fangs feel in the Ewe's throat? What could Blue have been thinking in the moment of her suffocation?

And Jasper was slashed by her own claws. Pertelote, too, has shed blood.

And Chalcedony: "Why mayn't I have children as any other Hen?" Chalcedony shall never know the motherhood born of her tender womb.

Shame. And who can survive such sorrows?

John Wesley maunders to the south. He goes without conviction. But if he didn't go, something inside him would cease to exist.

Might-be he gives up his soul by finding and fighting his dear Rooster. Would be like fighting himself. Might-be he dies by a slash of the Rooster's spur. Might-be he rips the wiggle-worms from his Lord Rooster. Well, and so.

The weather is malarial. John Wesley's heart is heavy laden.

Eurus, the Yellow-Eyed Wolf, has come to loath society. He despises these mealy-mouthed Creatures, the Meek who pretend to be warriors. Community? They deceive themselves. Ruled by bluster. Afraid of a damn Cock.

So Brown Eurus courses the outlands. Elk. Moose. Venison. He has better game to kill.

The corpse of the Char-Black Nota lies still unburied, but busy. For the nearly invisible Insects were quick to impregnate her dead flesh with masses of their myriad progeny. Fat little buntings which, when they hatch, will feed on her corpse as she has fed on others. They will enlighten her inward parts with a gentle amber glow.

String Jack has become a carving in marble.

The Animal's dread of the monstrous Wyrm had become the Animal's dread of Lord Chauntecleer.

PART FIVE

Pertelote and a
Psalm of Innocence

[Thirty-Nine]
Madness

Wyrm deliberate, Wyrm malefic! Wyrm who has destroyed good order and caused community to be divisible wiped out that past of playfulness. And the Rooster? Well, the Rooster has by some fierce reversal taken Wyrm's place.

John Wesley can smell the salt of the sea. But before he sees its waters he feels its breakers pounding the shore. Yet between the thunderous waves, in the wash of the wave's withdrawing, he hears a hissing.

Sing, says a voice.

And voices say, *What shall we sing?*

The voice says, *Immolation.*

And the voices answer, *Fires in the fabric of the Keepers. The conflagrations of the Lord.*

But when he reaches the salt sea, John Wesley finds no fires. He can make out a broad, dark, thick tar riding the swells, and nothing more.

Then like a cyclone a wind gets up and slams into the Weasel. Likewise, it tears pieces from the black island and flings them like rubber balls ashore.

Suddenly a an almighty crow dominates the wind and the waves: "*Consummatum est!* The bill is ended!"

Lord Chauntecleer! John sees the form of Lord Chauntecleer aloft and under the clouds, crowing a taunting Crow.

"Oh, taste my weapons, Surt! Though I come alone, though you may cinder my feathers and I die in your furnace, I shall first stab you and cut out your flaming heart, and you shall be quenched!"

At the zenith of his life and of all his flights, John Wesley thinks to himself, the Rooster sails in a whistling solitude, and he only, John Wesley Weasel, is here to witness his madness.

"Despair be damned! Come to me, O all ye powers! I am the Lord of vengeance! I shall be deified!"

Chauntecleer lays back his wings, balls his claws, and, like the Falcon, plummets.

[Forty]
Harmony

Ferric Coyote minces toward the Hemlock through a dismal, despoiled camp. Times past, he would have snapped into a spectacular freeze. Tonight it's Rachel's spirit in his breast. He steps around the bodies of insensate Creatures, seeking scraps to feed his daughters. He recognizes the death-scent everywhere. The corpses of his son and of his wife gave off a smell of spices. Here the scent is of corruptions.

Ferric has always loved the forests more than the plains. This tree is itself a forest. He leads Twill and Hopsacking under its boughs.

The plain Brown Bird flies down from darkness.

"Zicküt," she calls and leads Ferric to a form on the ground which is shaped like a dumdum.

The Coyote sits on his haunches and lowers his nose and crosses his eyes.

Ah. A Beetle. The plain Brown Bird has found a companion. And at the Beetle's back—what? For heaven's sake, it is a large, round dollop of poop.

The Beetle says, "Lazara, sir. Housekeeping."

Ferric frowns, because, what's a Lazara?

The Brown Bird says, "Zicküt."

The Beetle says, "Your friend the Bird tells me that your name is Ferric."

"Zicküt."

"And she tells me you are hungry."

Twill yaps, "Starving!"

Hopsacking seconds her sister: "Me too. Starving!"

Some of the inert animals begin to groan.

The Beetle leans back, twiddles her forelegs, parts her coverlets as if to fly, but calls with decorum, "My Lady?"

A tree branch shudders. Ice slides down the boughs outside.

Lazara repeats, "My Lady."

A Hen speaks in the limbs above: "No reason for greetings. But it isn't midnight, Lazara. It will never be midnight again."

"We've guests, my Lady."

The Hen says, "Lazara, we have become a charnel house."

The Black Beetle maintains her courtly timbre. "Obligations," she says, "are wanting."

The Lady Hen sighs, "Obligations. Obligations. Obligations."

"My Lady. Your guests are hungry."

The Hen is a spirit wandering the sands. "I am hungry for sunlight. I am hungry for sleep. I am hungry for summer, and the seasons, and the harvest, and righteousness. I am hungry for Chalcedony. O my God, I am hungry for—"

She would have said *Chauntecleer*, but the Coyote's sudden wailing. His sympathy has overflowed. He points his snout upward and howls a song of lamentation and bitter weeping for the woman who suffers on her perch.

Ferric's daughters join him. They raise pennywhistle voices and howl along.

The expressions of their own sorrows disturb the sleepers.

There is a general waking both outside and inside the Hemlock hall. Animals are listening, but they stay in their places. This is like no song they've ever heard.

Oh, for children lost and for innocence.

The littlest Creatures close their eyes and begin to rock. Birds bow their heads. The four-leggeds fold their paws together. And everyone in every voice begins to hum lows moans: *Mmmm*. A wordless, steady middle music: *Ahhh*. And the Coyote's wailing mounts the firmament.

In this moment the community have become the choirs come down from heaven. They are the music of the spheres. Their hearts cry out in a global harmony. They are one. It is a renewed blessing.

Pertelote, grateful for the reunion, breaks from her desolations and sings a benediction:

> "My loved ones, rest securely,
> For God this night must surely
> From peril guard your heads.
> Sweet slumbers he must send you,
> And bid his hosts attend you,
> And through the night watch o'er your beds"

[Forty-One]
'Love Wounds Me'

It has been a night of solace. Moreover, the day breaks warm.
So warm, in fact, that the sheath of ice that enclosed the
boughs of the Hemlock is melting, trickling down the needles.
Runnels of living water giggle along the ground.

Pertelote wakes to the water-music. In wonder she drops
from her limb and walks outside, and another water fills
her eyes.

Something cosmic has come to pass. The sun is shining!

Dear Lord God, the sun is shining, and the sky is blue.

"Lady Hen! Help me!"

Help who?

"John gots a Rooster what's a Rooster here!"

John Wesley Weasel!

Pertelote runs to the south side of the Hemlock. The
Weasel is striving backward, dragging a tarry body with his
fore-claws. Pertelote takes a position beside John Wesley.

"No wars," he grunts. "Is no wars, was no wars."

Pertelote reaches to John's burden and begins to comb the
tar away—then stops, shocked.

It's Chauntecleer! His eye is closed.

John says, "Salty waters, they shrivels little pinky worms. Worms outa the Rooster's eye, Worms outa the Rooster's nose and ears and mouth and feathers—all! Little maggots floats crispy like crackers."

Is he...? Is Chauntecleer alive?"

"Might be," says the Weasel.

The two of them lug their Rooster through fresh mud to the Hemlock.

"Chanty-cleer?" says Wodenstag. "Step-papa John, is it Chanty-cleer?"

Seven Mice spit on the Rooster. Seven Mice use their furry sides like rags and try to wash him.

The Mad House of Otter does a better job, and the Fawn De La Coeur still better. The Queen brings her Family Swarm, who cluster on the Rooster's body and work as if they were gathering pollen. One of them happens to sting Chauntecleer's comb, and the fallen Rooster twitches. His eye opens.

Pertelote thinks, What a beautiful iris. Why have I never seen that blossom in his eye before?

She murmurs, "Chauntecleer?"

His eye finds her.

"Pertelote."

"You have come home." She seeks to embrace her messy husband, but he draws back.

"No, no, I am not worthy."

She embraces him anyway.

He cries out. "Oh, how your love wounds me!"

"Wisht, wisht," Pertelote answers. "My love will heal you."

John Wesley says, "Lady Hen. John thinks the Rooster, he might-be dying."

"No, John! Don't say that!"

"John, he's a truth-teller."

Chauntecleer gargles in pain.

His wife's heart twists within her. "Somebody come!" she cries. "Somebody carry him out of the sun!"

It is Ferric Coyote who steps forth.

Chauntecleer sees him. Recognition destroys the Rooster. He begins to wail. "No, no, no, no, no—"

Ferric looks upon the Rooster without recrimination.

"Don't look at me!"

Ferric says, "Why?"

"Kill me instead!"

And Ferric says, "Why?"

"I killed your wife! It was me. I killed your son!"

"I know."

"I am so sorry, so sorry."

Pertelote says, "O my husband, do you know what you have done? Confessed. And your affliction is your penance. My sweet Chauntecleer, I love you. I love you. I have never *not* loved you."

"My God, who can forgive me now?" Having said that, Chauntecleer falters. He struggles against the tar. The Rooster is so exhausted.

Ferric Coyote says, "I forgive you."

John Wesley says, "John, he heaved you like a load. Was *his* forgivy-ness all right."

Pertelote says, "Don't leave us, Chauntecleer. You are good again. I want my good husband back. Don't leave me now."

A great lowing now fills the world. Soft with compassion the Dun Cow lows, "Almighty God forgives the sinner."

Chauntecleer is weeping. He opens his beak. His weeping becomes a long, long sigh. His eye closes, and he gives up his spirit.

[Forty-Two]
What Had Come to Pass

Out of the north there blew a great and mighty wind.

It stirred the clouds in heaven. It blasted them into flying scuds, then swept them clean away.

Dawn broke in the east.

The wind was an omnipotent tempest that lifted the blanket of Wyrm's ocean and rolled it back like a scroll.

It was from the summit of the cosmic mountain that this gale was rushing. The Dun Cow had elevated her head and had distended her nostrils. She breathed across the continents. She was an ungentle spirit. Her single horn was an ivory wand.

She did not reveal her purpose, not by her posture nor by in any aspect of her being. Simply, the Dun Cow is sovereign of the air.

Her breath was the vernal spring. Fimbul-winter cracked and perished. Seedlings sprouted.

[Forty-Three]
In Which Pertelote Sings a Memorial Song

After the wind ceased, the plain Brown Bird brought a winding sheet which she hasd knit with the needle of her beak. Together, she and Pertelote spread it over Chauntecleer's corpse.

Four Hens wrapped it closed, and seven Mice tucked it under.

The digging Animals had opened the tomb. The Family Swarm had sealed its sides and its floor with a sweetly scented wax.

And as the funeral procession moved to Chauntecleer's grave, Pertelote sang:

> "He woke me from my slumbering
> And taught softly how to sing
>   The songs.
> To him my mornings and that part
> Of me most holy—oh, my heart—
>   Belongs.

And who was bolder on the ground?
Or who more golden sailed around
   The skies?
Remember you? Oh, Lord, I will
Remember none but you until
   I die.

My dear, my dear,
My Chauntecleer."

Now available in eBook and paperback

The Third Book of the Dun Cow

Peace at the Last

Walter Wangerin Jr.

[Prologue]
Homeless

After the death of Lord Chauntecleer the Rooster, while the Beautiful Pertelote was still in mourning, spring burst open as if it had been swelling in the womb of the earth all through Fimbul-Winter.

Rain fell in torrents. The Mad House of Otter rejoiced, mud-slithering and cavorting and calling to one another and laughing because they said they looked like wet cigars.

The Queen Honey Bee and her Family Swarm buzzed abroad in search of blossoms dusted with pollen.

The Doe De La Coeur stayed in the hall under the boughs of the Hemlock tree. Her long legs would sink in the mud, and she'd be left stranded in an open field.

Likewise String Jack. He with all his friends and relations watched the heavy rainfall from under the eaves of the Hemlock, tisk-tisking at the Otters because the Otters were ruining shoots of young grass, and it was grass that the Rabbits wanted for food.

Sheep bowed their heads patiently. When other Animals came close to them they bleated warnings and begged them to go away. Sodden wool stinks, and stinking can embarrass a soft-hearted Sheep.

But hope had returned to the Animals. Slaughter had left them, please God, for good. Those Creatures who had learned to love the taste of blood had absconded: the yellow-eyed Wolf, gone; the Marten, after killing and eating the Grey Squirrel, gone; the fat Hen, who had proposed to eat a Ground Squirrel, gone; and the black Wolf, the red-eyed Wolf, dead.

And Wyrmesmere, that heaving sea, had been rolled back like a scroll. And Wyrm himself had been reduced to maggots.

John Wesley Weasel had decided to take the Brothers Mice under his wing, as it were. It was his notion to turn them into a militia as grim as he himself was grim.

"File single!" he commanded.

When the brothers had flipped into their places, Wodenstag first, Samstag last, the Weasel faced them. "Mices! Count off!"

"One," squeaked Wodenstag. "Two!" This was Donnertag. Freitag was just about to squeak "Three," but the Weasel interrupted:

"John, he can'ts *hear* you!"

So Freitag threw out his tiny chest and squeak-roared, "Step-papa! Three!"

Dienstag, Samstag, Sonntag, Montag all squeak-boomed, "Four! Five! Six! Seven."

John Wesley turned his back to them and cried, "Forwards, harch!"

Spring eased Pertelote's grief. And just as well. In Chauntecleer's absence someone must take his Animals into her care. She sang Matins. She sang every one of the Canonical Crows:

> "My darlings, sweet the sunrise, soft
> The dawning, good the eve when falls
>   The dusk.
>
> Work the daylong, sleep the night through,

Dream of him who still requires your
    Trust."

So it was in those days when spring was filled with promises.
And so it might have gone for the rest of the Animals' lives.

But the spring that smiles is the season that must also frown.
Nothing exists without its opposite. Light needs darkness to
prove that it *is* light. Day needs night. Heat needs cold. Health
needs disease. Joy needs suffering. And life cannot be measured
unless it is by death.

Black clouds swelled over the land. Wind blew the rain like
pellets into the Creatures' faces. Creatures took cover under the
Hemlock. Thunder rolled, and lightning stuttered closer and
closer on spiders' legs, until a single firebolt struck the pinnacle
of the Hemlock tree. Immediately its needles spat and sparked.
And, in spite of the rain, its boughs burst into flame.

Pertelote was horrified but not dumbfounded. She cried
out. She raised her cry to the level of an outright Crow. The
mighty crash of the lightning and the fire in the crown of their
tree had sent the Animals not rushing out, but huddling around
the trunk of the Hemlock.

Pertelote called John Wesley Weasel, who saw their rank
stupidity and bombed the Animals with his body.

"Mices!" he roared. "File single!"

Their step-papa's command emboldened seven little hearts.

"Hup! Hup! Nip Buggars in their butts!'

The military Mice obeyed. Hens began to cackle and run.
Ferric Coyote, who would have hunkered down and fixed
himself into a desperate freeze, yiped and ran. His daughters
followed him out and across the mud.

The Weasel tore fur from the Jackrabbits' backs.

Then Pertelote brought order to John Wesley's galloping
mess. She gathered the Animals into ranks and led them away
from the Hemlock. Under black clouds the tree was a shooting

candlestick. Its blaze reflected in the Animals' eyes. It cast a lurid light over their faces. Pertelote herself seemed a firebrand as she flew back and forth, under the tree and out again, making sure that no one had been left behind.

Chauntecleer was dead. The Hemlock was dying. When every Animal had been accounted for, and Pertelote had alighted beside John Wesley, her emotions overwhelmed her. What were they going to do now? No focus for a home. No purpose but survival. No season that was not untrustworthy.

The trunk of the Hemlock did not burn. Rather, it became a singular, smoking spire, and then a black obelisk, a memorial to civilizations past.